MIND GAMES

Cecilia Tan

raVenous
romance ™

RS

RED SILK
EDITIONS

First published in paperback in 2010 by
Red Silk Editions
an imprint of Red Wheel/Weiser, LLC
500 Third Street, Suite 230
San Francisco, CA 94107

First published as an e-book in 2009 by
Ravenous Romance
100 Cummings Center
Suite 123A
Beverly, MA 01915
www.ravenousromance.com

ISBN: 978-1-59003-204-6

Cover design by April Martinez
Cover photograph © Literary Partners Group, Inc.

Printed in Canada
TCP
10 9 8 7 6 5 4 3 2 1

Dedication

To Corwin, my true love for 17 years (so far)

Acknowledgments

Thanks to Lori Perkins: Every word of encouragement from you seems to turn into a book! To Marsha Philitas for excellent advice. To Nina Harper for cheerleading, encouragement, and being a role model for me. To Corwin for much inspiration, as well as cooking so many fabulous dinners while I was writing this, as well as for never complaining about how much time the writing took. To my LiveJournal friends for everything, and especially my first readers: Patrick, dba, Marion, Lisa, Jean Roberta, and Eric. Thanks also to Bethany and Cynthia, my assistants at Circlet Press, without whose efforts I never would have had the mental capacity (or time) to actually write this book.

Chapter One

"COME ON, Wren, I know you're in there!"

Wren Delacourt hugged the pillow over her ears, but there was no chance Lawrence was going to go away. Just last night, she'd told him to come by at noon today, and he'd seen her go into her unit in the condo, and if she didn't get up soon, he was going to start to worry that something terrible had happened to her....

No. Best not to think about that sort of thing. "I'm coming," she called, but weakly. No way he'd hear that through her bedroom door and across the kitchen. She had to sit up, then stand up, then open the door. She felt on the floor for her bathrobe.

Halfway to the door, she had to stop and put her hands to her eyes. The world seemed too *hot*. Not the actual temperature, which was pleasant enough, but it was as if something electrical were pricking at her, about to overheat like a transformer.

Or maybe it was just a hangover. She pulled open the door and saw Lawrence's expression fall.

"Oh my God, are you all right?" he blurted.

She must have looked a fright; Lawrence was never tactless. She leaned on the door frame. "Do I have raccoon eyes?" she asked, examining her palms for mascara smudges.

"You do," he said, pushing her gently into the apartment, "if a raccoon were run over by a school bus three or four times." He was carrying a paper bag and a wonderful smell came from it. "Go on now, why don't you get washed up and I'll squeeze some oranges?"

Wren did as she was told. Lawrence was a good neighbor and a good friend and she was glad she wasn't alone just now, even if he didn't know why she was such a wreck. She went into the bathroom and washed her face, finally giving in and using some cold cream to help remove the eyeliner and mascara. The waterproof kind was more trouble than it was worth, she decided, since it practically refused to come off even with goop. She ran a comb through her hair, still not used to how short it was. The cut was what her hairdresser had called "boyishly chic" and Wren thought it made her look a little like Winona Ryder. At the very least it made her eyes look huge, now that they weren't hidden under black bangs.

She slipped back into the bedroom to pull on some sweatpants and a clean shirt, then emerged to find that Lawrence, as promised, had squeezed juice for them both and had set out a few fresh-baked pastries. She sat down at the counter and bit into a chocolate croissant, still warm. "Decadence," she said.

He chuckled. "The fresh fruit is the decadent part for me. In Europe, croissants and chocolate grow on trees."

She poked him. Lawrence had only a trace of a British accent but liked to act like he was fresh off the Mayflower. "I've been to England. They had oranges and orange juice there."

"At exorbitant prices. Maybe the conversion to the pound made it not so obvious to you." He took a cheese Danish and ate in silence for a bit before venturing to ask, "Bad date?"

"You could say that," she said in a quiet voice, while she decided what to tell him. "Not that kind, though." She'd told him plenty of disaster stories about men before, but this wasn't one of those times, and she decided Lawrence could handle the truth without turning into a blithering idiot. "It's the anniversary of when my parents died. I went to visit their gravesite yesterday." She gave a little shrug, as if to say it was no big deal.

Lawrence took a sip of his juice. "I didn't know your parents were dead," he said, without undue emotion.

"Yeah, when I was a teenager." Wren shrugged again. "Car accident. My sister was only ten. She took it harder than I did."

Of course, that was all a massive oversimplification, but she really didn't want to get into it. Lawrence nodded and continued eating without pushing her to say anything more.

Which was probably why she did. "I usually see her there. At their grave, I mean. We don't talk much, but she hasn't returned my calls for like four months. Her e-mail bounces, but you know people change addresses. But—" She looked up from her juice to see Lawrence looking at her with a thoughtful expression on his face.

"You think something might have happened to her?"

"Yeah, I'm starting to worry. I mean, I wasn't really that worried, but...she wouldn't have forgotten this." Wren looked out the small kitchen window. From here, all she could see was a little bit of the Japanese maple tree across the street, and a red minivan almost the same color as the maple's leaves. "I suppose I could file a missing persons report with the police, at least."

Lawrence finished his Danish and licked his fingertips like a cat washing its paws. "It couldn't hurt. Even if it does turn out she's just...making a change or something. From what you've told me, she's not exactly the most constant person?"

"I know." It was one of the reasons they didn't talk much or see each other much. Abby was prone to new fads, new hobbies, new schemes to make money, new boyfriends...so much so that Wren wasn't even sure she'd recognize her sister from visit to visit. They tended to see each other at Aunt Brenda's for Christmas, have lunch around their birthdays in April, and now it was September, when they either went together to the burial site, or would meet there. Wren never knew if Abby would be blonde, brunette, bisexual, or born-again. "It's like every few months she tries to become some new person, as if *this* time she grows up, it'll bring our parents back or something."

Lawrence shrugged. "Maybe she decided to give up."

Wren shrugged back. "I'll call the police later. The more I think about it now, the more I think she's probably just joined a tree-hugging cult or something and doesn't know what day it is."

* * * *

A week later, Wren had still not called the police and she wasn't sure why. Just a feeling she couldn't shake. She went to work in the mornings at the university, where she spent her days scanning and transcribing the rare books collection, and was home by five-thirty. Then it was forty-five minutes on the treadmill while watching TV, some dinner, and then more TV or a book until she fell asleep. The sum total of her excitement was that someone out there seemed to have gotten her cell phone number by mistake, and she kept seeing missed calls from Number Unavailable.

At first she'd thought, *could it be Abby?* But when she finally managed to answer one of the calls, when she wasn't deep in the library, it had been some guy claiming he was calling as a result of her personal ad and she sounded nice, could they meet for tea? She hung up. Part of her said, *hey, he sounded kind of nice, too.* What if it was fate that he dialed the wrong number and that was how they met and wouldn't that make a lovely "how we met" story for later?

But no. She started keeping the phone in silent mode in case the number *was* actually printed wrong in the paper and he wouldn't be the only caller. Otherwise, it was a boring week of the routine. She'd gotten a note under her door about scheduling some kind of utility inspection, but had ignored it, not wanting to sit home on a Saturday waiting for some guy to show up.

Not that she went anywhere, though perhaps she should have. On the weekend she had more quiet time, and the feeling nagged her as she watered her plants and vacuumed the rug in a vain attempt to stay busy. Call the police? Don't call the police? Why should it be such a big deal?

But each time she convinced herself to just call, by the time she got her cell phone out of her bag, something in her had decided she wouldn't.

Just a feeling. But despite what everyone had said, despite all evidence to the contrary, Wren still listened to her feelings.

It was one of the things she and Abby had fought about. When they were kids, Wren used to tell her things that were going to happen. Sometimes wonderful things, like when the first snow was going to fall, or where to find a lost kitten in the woods. Sometimes awful things, like Uncle Herbert's heart attack, or when City Hall was going to catch fire.

She'd stopped telling her parents about her feelings after the fearful and pained looks they'd tried to hide, and after they'd brought her to a child psychologist when she was five. She managed to get out of having to go back to the psychologist, but only by not speaking about those things again. But after a few years, Abby was old enough to talk to, and her sister had been the one to hear all of Wren's predictions, sometimes with delight, sometimes with dread, sometimes claiming she didn't want to know, other times asking her to answer questions for her. Would nine-year-old Bobby Calandra say yes if she asked him to go to the County Fair with her? Would Mrs. Peabody find out if she cheated on her math test? Would Daddy say yes if she asked him to get another cat?

Wren couldn't always answer, and Abby would accuse her of faking the whole thing if she didn't answer—or if she didn't like the answer she got.

The worst came when Wren didn't predict what would happen to their parents. She'd been thirteen, just starting her last year of middle school, when disaster had struck. She hadn't seen it coming, but then she didn't predict everything, didn't know what was going to happen to every person every minute of the day. And even if she'd had a premonition of some kind, what would she have done? Begged and pleaded with her parents not to get in the car? Even at that age, she knew her premonitions could land herself in the nuthouse. And then there would have been no one to take care of Abby.

But Abby didn't see it that way.

Just thinking about it made Wren feel tired. But when Wren had a feeling, she trusted it. She wiped out the inside of the microwave, thinking it over.

If she really trusted her intuition, and her intuition said not to call the police, then could her intuition help her find Abby somehow?

Stupid idea. Crazy idea. She hadn't actively tried to ask for the answer to a question since she was eleven or so. At the time she'd made a game out of it, convincing her sister to sneak her a piece of chocolate out of her mother's stash above the refrigerator, and to steal a sip of Schnapps out of the liquor cabinet in the Dixie cup.

Come to think of it, that was the time she'd predicted Uncle Herbert's heart attack. Abby had wanted to know what he was getting her for Christmas, and Wren still remembered the sick feeling she'd had in her stomach as she knew with all certainty he wasn't going to live that long.

Some things, she had realized then, she really didn't want to know.

On the other hand, hiding from what had happened to Abby, if anything, wasn't going to help. Some things were scary *not* to know.

"Oh, screw it," she said, and went to change her clothes. It was only three in the afternoon, but Wren didn't feel she had to wait until sundown. The booze and chocolate probably weren't even necessary, but if she wanted to try to repeat what she'd done as a child, there was always the stash of gourmet chocolate bars in the kitchen for "emergencies," like really bad PMS. She got out a bar of dark chocolate and broke off a piece. Her kitchen table was a counter-height and did double duty as a cutting board stand when she cooked anything elaborate. She set the piece of chocolate on a napkin on the table, and then dug through the cabinet.

Last week, after the visit to her parents, she'd finished the half bottle of wine that had been sitting there for months, since that Italian meal Lawrence had cooked. What else did she have? Hmm, there was a bottle of dry sherry she used sometimes for cooking, an unopened bottle of coconut rum she had gotten as a door prize and didn't think she'd like, and a small open bottle of port, which she had bought to use in a sauce.

It would do. She poured a little into a glass and set it next to the chocolate.

What else? She sat at the table, her hands on the butcher block, and took a deep breath. Nothing else came to mind.

Well, here goes nothing, she thought. She swallowed the port, then took a bite of the chocolate, letting it melt on her tongue. Her eyes drifted closed. It was good chocolate.

She wasn't aware of her mind having gone quiet until she started to think again. It was a bit like falling asleep and not realizing you had until you jerked awake. Only in her case, it was as if she started to dream.

Going down a set of stairs, like into a bar or nightclub. The too-sweet scent of disinfectant, hiding a more raw smell. Following a man with long red hair, starkly copper-colored against the black leather of his jacket.

Hands already bound behind her back. A rising sense of fear as she followed him. Down a narrow hallway, the light dim. Someone else following behind, making sure she followed.

Then rough hands pushing her, through a door, into darkness, the hands forcing her to her knees, and then the salty bulk in her mouth....

Wren jerked, sending the glass flying. It shattered against the tile floor and she was startled to see the shards glittering in the afternoon sunlight. It felt as if for those moments she'd actually been somewhere else, someplace where it was night. She could almost still smell the cleaning products in the air.

She rested her forehead on her hand. She'd never had a vision like that before. Was that something that had already happened? Or was going to?

Were those Abby's eyes she had seen through?

She eased her way out of the kitchen to get the vacuum cleaner, but found herself at her desk with her phone in her hand. Whether what she had seen was the past or the future, Abby was in trouble. The police would never take something like this seriously, though.

She opened her laptop and did a search for private investigators instead.

For whatever reason, the listing for Derek Chapman caught her eye. Perhaps it was that the first thing next to his name said "Missing Persons" and not "Cheating Spouses"—

although she didn't really register that until she was already calling his number.

She got his answering machine. "Uh, hi, yes, Mr. Chapman. My name is Wren Delacourt and I think my sister is missing and wondered if you could help. I last heard from her four months ago. Um, I don't know what else to say?" She left her number and hung up.

* * * *

A traffic jam outside the big church on Springfield Avenue slowed Wren's progress. She'd forgotten it was Sunday, forgotten to go around the other way. The policeman directing traffic in and out of the church parking lot seemed to eye her suspiciously as she inched past instead of turning in. But although she felt she was doing the right thing, going to meet with Mr. Chapman instead of calling the police, her head kept telling her it didn't make sense.

She pulled into the parking lot behind the post office and made her way to the building. It was locked on a Sunday, but she pressed the doorbell and the door buzzed. She took the elevator to the second floor, as he'd told her to on the phone.

He'd sounded very nice. Very kind. Not as gruff or tough as she'd imagined he would, but then her ideas of what a private investigator would be like came from movies and TV shows. She clutched her purse in both hands as she read the signs on the offices. An accountant, tax preparation... aromatherapy? That door was more colorfully decorated than the others.

The open door at the end of the hall had to be his. He probably had spoken so kindly to her because he was humoring her, she thought suddenly. But she hadn't told him the weird part yet.

Wren urged herself through the door and found herself face to face with a dark-haired young man. He was neatly dressed in a turtleneck and a windbreaker and she wondered for a second whether Mr. Chapman had a personal assistant. "I'm here to meet Mr. Chapman?"

He laughed, and his smile was warm. "I'm Chapman. You can call me Derek, if you like, Miss Delacourt."

"Wren," she said, holding out her hand.

His palm was warm even if the handshake was brief. He gestured toward an empty chair and then, to her surprise, sat next to her instead of going around the other side of the desk. The office wasn't large, but there also didn't seem to be much in it. One file cabinet behind the desk. A small table with old newspapers on it. "Wren, like the bird?" he asked.

"Yes, yes exactly." She was feeling more and more comfortable with him by the second. She sat with her purse on her lap, her suit skirt too short for her to properly cross her legs, but she had worn it to try to make a good impression. "Most people think I'm trying to shorten Renee, or something. Um, thanks for agreeing to meet me on a Sunday."

He shrugged. "I don't exactly work regular hours. So you said on the phone you're looking for your sister?"

"Yes." She took a deep breath. Where to start? Wren picked something concrete. "She hasn't returned my phone calls for about four months. Maybe two months ago, her voice mailbox got full. Now when I call, I get a message that sounds like she hasn't paid her bill. And her e-mail bounces."

He nodded. "And have you talked to other family members about her?"

Wren deflated. "The only person she keeps in touch with besides me is our Aunt Brenda, and by keep in touch I mean Aunt Brenda sends her a Christmas card every year, and Abby—that's my sister—shows up at her house Christmas Day. I didn't want to call Brenda. It seemed like tattling on Abby. Well, unless she's really in trouble. Or...I don't know."

"It's okay," Derek said, and his voice was soft. "I'm going to start taking some notes, if that's all right with you."

An hour later, Wren had told him all about Abby's tendencies to flit from one thing to another, one job to another, one relationship to another. Wren hadn't even been sure what her last address was since she'd mentioned moving back in April but had never given her the new address. And Wren told him about the fights they'd had, their parents, all of it. He listened, and he listened well, and oh, it felt so good to just tell someone about it and not try to pick and choose which parts to hide.

But now she'd come to it. The part about why she'd called him, when he finally asked if she'd notified the police.

She was looking at her hands, her neatly trimmed nails lined up on the top of her purse like birds on a wire, and not at him when she said, "My intuition said not to. I kept thinking I should, but...I did a silly thing."

He said nothing, but waited for her to explain.

"I decided to see if I could find out for myself what happened to her. So I tried to do it like when we were kids—we had a kind of magic spell or ritual we'd do, with chocolate and breaking into the liquor cabinet. I don't know if that was important or if it was just an excuse to be naughty." She could feel herself blushing, but she went on. "Anyway, I had a little port, and some chocolate, and then...I had a vision."

Her voice was so soft by the end of her sentence she wondered if he could even hear it. "Maybe it was just, I dunno, a sick fantasy or something. But it was like I dreamed I was her. And these men were taking me somewhere dark, and my hands were tied behind my back, and...."

Wren put her hand over her mouth, remembering the smell of the air and the taste of the flesh that had probed her mouth. She kept her eyes open though, as if the sight of Derek's bare-bones office might dispel the vision.

"Would you like a glass of water?" he asked, looking concerned but not freaked out. "You've been talking a long time."

Wren swallowed, trying to stop hyperventilating. "Yes, yes, that would be very nice." But when he moved to stand up, she put her hand on his arm, holding him there. "No, wait. Please just stay here with me."

"All right." He settled in his chair again.

She took a deeper breath and let it out slowly. "I don't know if what I saw was the past, the future, or what. I...broke it off before I learned anything more. But it just makes me more worried for her."

He nodded. "Understandably so."

"Do you believe me?"

He put his hand over hers, and she realized she'd never pulled her own away. "It doesn't matter what I believe. Could it be your imagination conjuring up something to worry about? Maybe. Could your subconscious have put together clues from something she said to you or things you gathered without realizing? Sure. Could you really be psychic? Could be. None of those things matters. If you're hiring me to find your sister, I'll use any information I can."

His eyes seemed very large and round as he said this to her, and Wren found herself feeling calmer again. Much calmer, although her heart seemed to still want to beat out of her chest. She slipped her hand back then, and said simply, "Thank you. And yes, you're hired."

* * * *

Wren invited Lawrence over to watch a DVD that night, and they ordered a pizza and watched *Moonstruck*, which Lawrence professed was one of his favorite films. "For a gay man, you sure do seem to go for these hot romantic comedies," she said as he slipped the disc into the player.

She found herself watching the movie in a daze, though, thinking about Derek Chapman and the way his hand had felt touching hers. People in the movies always seemed to have such Big Love that Wren felt like if it were real, it would eat her alive like a giant turtle. She didn't even like to fantasize about it. Lawrence, on the other hand, had an endless appetite for romances, whether in the news, in the movies, or in his imagination. He'd had about as many successful dates as Wren, which was to say not many, but he dreamed of meeting The Right One.

She hoped he would, even if he forgot all about her when it swept him away.

They called it an early night since both of them had work in the morning, and Wren got into bed and lay there looking at the stripe of light on the ceiling from the street lamp outside. She was restless and went to the window, looking out on the neighborhood. Most of the houses were dark, everyone sleeping. Under the streetlamp the red minivan at the curb looked brown, the color leached from it. If she'd had a diary, she might have written about Derek. But what would she have said? *Dear Diary, Met a man today. He's got very kind eyes.*

She hadn't said a word to Lawrence about him.

Sleep claimed her eventually and in the morning, when her dreams were always the most vivid, she found herself moving through a dark passageway. Her hands were behind her back, but her mind had blurred the details. It was like the vision and yet it wasn't, and she was herself in the dream, she was sure of that. The man behind her herded her into a small room and closed the door. They were alone there, the ceiling low as if it were a basement room, and she went gratefully to her knees as if the weight of the building above her had been pressing down on her.

She couldn't see him. He was behind her. But she could feel his hands on her shoulders, petting them soothingly. "Wren," he whispered. "Do you know what sex is?"

She felt her lip tremble as she mustered her answer. "Do you mean, like did I have sex ed in school? Or is that 'know' in the biblical sense?"

"I know you're not a virgin, but you may as well be," came the soft, warm voice, thick and sweet as honey. "I meant philosophically. Metaphorically and literally, sex is entry."

Had she been naked this whole time? Perhaps she had. She shivered as his finger traced a line from her chin down her throat, over one nipple, and between her legs. He circled her clit, counting each movement as if tallying up what she owed. "One, two, three, four, five."

He stopped at ten and then slid lower. She could feel the roughness of his clothes against her back, his breath against her neck. His other hand was flat against her belly, while his index finger sought her wetness.

He slid his finger in the slickness there, sawing back and forth over her sensitive nub, but never quite putting his finger into her. "Six, seven, eight, nine, ten."

She trembled.

"Entry," he said again, a whisper in her ear. "Penetration. It doesn't matter what part of me enters what part of you. Once I'm inside, I'm inside."

She tried to speak, to say something, but she couldn't very well argue with that recitation of facts, could she? It was true.

"Eleven, twelve, thirteen, fourteen. Does that feel good, Wren?"

She nodded. She had never been a good liar, especially not in dreams. "Why...why are my hands tied?" she finally asked.

"Shackled by your repression," came the reply with a chuckle, as one slim finger began to press inward.

"Then be our tenth caller and you could win an all-expense paid vacation to Jamaica!"

Her body jerked at the harsh, loud voice. Oh God, the *radio*. Her alarm.

As she turned her head toward the clock radio, Wren found her neck damp with sweat and her hand in her panties. She pulled it out quickly, turning off the radio and hurrying into the shower.

Such a strange dream. A mystery man whose face she never saw, whose voice she could barely hear most of the time, touching her that way. It should have disturbed her more than it did, except all she could think of was washing the smell and sweat away. She held the shower sprayer between her legs and nearly collapsed in the tub as she came.

She dried off sitting on the toilet lid, her legs still shaking, and then everything began to seem more disturbing. Was it a coincidence the dream came the night after she'd met an attractive man? Was it a warning? It hadn't felt like a warning, and it hadn't felt like Derek in the dream, either.

She shook her head. Sometimes a dream was just a dream, after all.

Wren looked up suddenly. How long had she been in the shower, then sitting there wool-gathering? She was going to be late for the Monday morning meeting. She pulled on clothes quickly and nearly ran out the door, happy not for the first time that her super-short hairdo needed no prep time at all. She combed it at a red light on her way to work.

She didn't even realize that she'd left her cell phone sitting by the computer, or that its message light was blinking.

Chapter Two

WREN STOPPED at the market on her way home to get a pre-cooked chicken, so it was after six o'clock when she pulled her car into her space behind the condo. She wasn't sure where time went in the market; no matter how little she bought, it always seemed to take an hour to get out of there.

Carrying the bag in her arms, she caught the aroma of the roast chicken wafting up as she made her way to the back door. She fumbled with her keys a bit, but got the door open, and was climbing the stairs up to her unit when she realized she could hear her own doorbell ringing. Looking behind her to the front door, she could see the outline of someone's head in the frosted glass window that was shaped like the upper half of a wagon wheel.

When she pulled open the door, she saw Derek there, and an "oh!" was startled right out of her.

"Miss...Wren. Sorry to drop in on you like this, but you haven't been answering your phone." His face and voice were serious but not horribly grim, she thought.

Still, she steeled herself for bad news. "What happened?"

He glanced from side to side. "May I come in? I'm sorry if it's not convenient, but I was driving by here on my way home and thought I'd check to see if you were free to talk. Lots of people lose their cell phones or their batteries die...."

Wren blushed. "I hardly use mine. I'm not used to getting calls. It's probably dead in the bottom of my purse." She realized she'd never turned the ringer back on after switching it to silent mode after the stray "personal ad" call. She backed up a step. He couldn't be there to tell her Abby was dead. He wouldn't be so calm. Would he? "Come on in. Have you eaten? I've got a whole chicken in here."

He didn't answer the question, but he did follow her into her kitchen and didn't protest when she set out plates and glasses for both of them.

She clucked her tongue. "Here it is." Her phone was sitting in plain sight on the desk, the little green light on it blinking impatiently. "Water? Tea? Orange juice? I've got fizzy water."

"Fizzy water would be great," he said. "And you can delete the messages from me. I've got more to tell you now anyway."

She slipped the phone into her pocket and poured seltzer for both of them, pulling vegetables out of the fridge when she put the bottle back. "Should I be sitting down while you talk, or can I make a salad?"

He stood. "Why don't you sit, and I'll make the salad? I don't want you to cut yourself if you find my news startling."

Wren blinked. "And here I was telling myself you couldn't be so calm if...if it was something really bad."

He steered her to a stool at the tall table for two, and moved her seltzer closer to her as if to suggest she drink. Or maybe just to remind her it was there. "Just listen and then you tell me if you think it's bad, okay?"

He brought the carrots and red onion and cherry tomatoes to the cutting board and set to cutting them up as he talked. "The first thing I did after you left yesterday was look up some information about your sister on the Internet. There wasn't much there. Her old phone listings. Her name in an online newsletter she helped out with a couple of years ago, that sort of thing."

Wren nodded and sipped at the seltzer, the bubbles tickling her nose.

"I did manage to figure out where she'd moved after the address you gave me. I figured I'd go by there, just to check it out. It was a small apartment building a couple of blocks from the park, toward the river. Not a bad neighborhood. I drove by late last night, but when I got there, I found the front door boarded shut. From the look of the brick, there had been a fire, and the building was condemned."

"Oh no," Wren found herself saying, gripping the glass tight.

"I had to wait until first thing this morning to get to the police reports about the fire. It doesn't look like your sister was there at the time. The only fatality reported was the landlord. Four people were treated for smoke inhalation in the hospital and released: none of them was your sister. The fire is flagged as a possible arson, but if the landlord was responsible, well, he paid the price. The police wanted to interview all the residents about it, but it doesn't appear they ever talked to your sister. She might have moved in with a friend or something after that and they don't have any record of it. Is there lettuce? Or do you just prefer the non-greens?"

His question seemed to bring her back to the kitchen from the world of her imagination, trying to picture Abby fleeing a burning building and never looking back. "Oh, there's pre-washed spinach in the crisper. And dressing in the door."

He nodded, putting a handful of leaves on each of their plates, topping them with the chopped vegetables, and then drizzling them with bottled dressing. He put the dressing away and returned with the chicken, still in its tray. Steam rose as he lifted the cover off. "Anything else you would like?" he asked, "or are you eating low carb?"

Wren couldn't help but smile. "No, I'm just too lazy and hungry to make any. I'll eat a carby breakfast to make up for it." She used her knife and fork to take one of the legs of the chicken. "So, is that it? The trail's gone cold?"

He took a bite of salad on his fork and chewed thoughtfully for a moment. "There are some other avenues to try. I won't give up just yet, if you don't want me to."

The chicken was warm and salty. Wren resisted the urge to pick up the drumstick in her fingers in front of a house-guest, and instead tore pieces off the thigh with her fork. The meat was so soft she didn't even need the knife. "If you could keep looking a bit more," she said quietly, "that would be great. I mean, if her place burned, I could see her just starting over and never looking back. Maybe even a new phone, new everything? And just letting the old bills pile up. That's the sort of thing she'd do. Like the fire would automatically get her off scot-free of any responsibility."

They ate in silence for a bit, then Derek asked, quiet and serious, "And do you feel like she's your responsibility?"

"Yes!" Wren was surprised at the vehemence of her own outburst. "Yes, I do!" She hadn't really thought of it that way, not in so many words, but there it was. "Especially since she doesn't take responsibility for herself."

She expected Derek to argue, to point out that her sister was a grown woman, or something. But he just looked at her, then back at his plate as he tried to spear a cherry tomato on his fork. "I'll keep looking," he said, when he caught it. "I'm working on another missing person right now, too, but that doesn't keep me very busy."

Wren found herself very curious about how a private investigator made a living, since he couldn't possibly be living off what she and one other person were paying him, could he? But she wasn't the prying type. She finished her meal in silence, and then looked on in shock as Derek put the leftover chicken away, took the dishes to the sink, rinsed them and put them in the dishwasher, then brought a damp sponge back to the table to wipe up the grease spot left by the chicken container.

"What?" he asked when he realized she was staring at him as if he'd grown two heads.

"You must be some kind of neat freak," she said, holding back a laugh. "I've never seen a guy wipe up. One or two who thought they were God's gift for loading the dishwasher, but never one who used a sponge."

He chuckled, then went to put the sponge back in the sink while Wren got up to see if there was ice cream in the freezer. "My mother taught me how to cook and how to clean up," Derek said. "She was very particular about a lot of things, and she couldn't do them herself because she was disabled.

After my dad died, it was just the two of us in the house all my teen years. She died just after I got to college."

"Oh." Wren wondered if that was how she sounded when she talked about her own family tragedy. As if she'd practiced it, said it so many times that it would come out sounding nonchalant, as if she were talking about the weather. It was just a fact. But for Wren, telling people *anything* was a big deal.

She put her hand over his. "Thank you for telling me."

"You're welcome." His eyes met hers. "Any reason you have the freezer open?"

She shut it with another "oh," thinking she had said that a lot tonight. "Just hoping for some ice cream. There isn't any, though. I should have picked some up."

He glanced at his watch. "We could walk over to the place on Main. It's only five or six blocks and it's not that chilly out."

Wren regarded him. "Yeah, we could." Why not? She didn't have anything better to do, and he was nice. "It's not against some kind of client appropriateness rules or something?"

"Getting ice cream?" He laughed. "No. That's not mentioned in the Private Dick Handbook. If you're really concerned...we can go Dutch."

She laughed. "Okay." She grabbed her purse, threw on a jacket, and then held the door open for him.

They met Lawrence coming in the front door. Wren looked back and forth between the two of them for a moment, trying not to show any embarrassment on her face, then said, "Lawrence, meet my friend, Derek. Derek, my downstairs neighbor, Lawrence."

Lawrence's eyebrows perched high up his forehead as he shook Derek's hand, clearly surprised or maybe even skeptical. "Nice to meet you." He looked back at Wren, curiosity burning in his eyes. "Catching a movie?"

Wren resisted the urge to shrug or to grab Derek's hand and pull him down the front steps. "No, going to get some ice cream. See you later!" She went down the steps herself instead, hoping that was enough of a hint for Lawrence not to invite himself along.

She waited until they were a block away to say to Derek, "Sorry about that. I didn't tell him I was hiring someone to look for Abby, and if you'd said something about it, it would have looked like I'm hiding it from him."

Derek's eyebrow tilted. "Aren't you?"

She huffed. "Well, I didn't mean to be. But I haven't told him yet, and now I'm going to have to, or he's going to be all over whether we are dating or something. He's my best friend, but that doesn't mean I always want his opinion on everything." Well, except she usually did, especially when dates went wrong. But, she reminded herself, this wasn't a date, and nothing had gone wrong.

Derek chuckled. "You're not comfortable keeping secrets."

"Not really, no. I'm not good at keeping track of who was told what. I just don't like hurting people's feelings."

"And you think he'd be hurt that you didn't tell him about me?"

"Maybe." She stuck her hands in her jacket pockets, leaves swirling around her ankles as they walked. "He's a good friend," she said, and left it at that.

They were nearly there when Derek asked, "Do you have a photograph of your sister I could borrow? Or that you could e-mail to me?"

"Sure. Aunt Brenda emailed a picture of the two of us together last Christmas, actually. I'm sure it's in my computer somewhere." She had meant to get it printed out and framed to put on her desk, but hadn't gotten around to it. She found herself praying that it wouldn't take on a new meaning, but tried to put aside the worry. "Now, chocolate, strawberry, pistachio?"

"Let's see what they have," he said, holding the door open for her.

* * * *

The next day, when she got to her work station in the back of the library, she found a single white flower in a vase sitting there. No card, no note. Later, when she quizzed the student working the front desk, all she could say was that some guy had dropped it off. It was a calla lily, just one long graceful throat in a tall vase of heavy glass, somewhat phallic in shape, now that she considered it.

Oh, God. She felt a flush as she thought about Derek. It had to be from him, right? It was elegant and yet sexy at the same time.

She shook herself while her equipment booted up. But Derek had been every inch the gentleman, maintaining, she thought, a professional distance. Just because he seemed so sympathetic and so caring, and just because she was hard up and apparently horny, her brain had turned him into her new fantasy lust object.

She looked again for a card, but didn't find one. So if it was from him, she didn't know why he would have sent it. And if it wasn't from him, then who was it from?

She put it out of her mind until lunch when she walked out to the dining hall to get some soup and a salad. She had just set her tray down at a table when her phone rang. She pulled it out of her pocket immediately, thinking it might be Derek.

"Hi, Wren?"

Was that him? She pressed one hand over her ear. "Hello?"

"Wren, it's Steve."

"Who?"

"Er, sorry, look, please don't hang up." He sounded pathetic, like a lost puppy. "I work on the campus, too. I'm just really shy. I...I know some of your co-workers, but I hate blind dates and I bet you do, too."

She sat down. "Wait a second, are you saying we've got mutual friends who wanted to fix us up, but you wouldn't let them, so instead you're calling me yourself?"

"Well, yeah." Wren wasn't sure, but she thought maybe she heard him swallow. Then he continued quickly, "But really, we did meet once at a department thing. Well, maybe meet is too strong a word, since I was afraid to talk to you."

"But you're not afraid now?" This guy didn't make a whole lot of sense, but at the same time, neither did much about sex or love or dating to Wren, so maybe he was just as confused as she was.

"Well, the phone is a little easier. But I'd really like to just have coffee or something. Or tea? At the Student Union's even fine with me, though there are some nicer places, like maybe the Starbucks across from the science center? Like, after work?"

She knew the place he meant. "You mean today?"

He paused and she could imagine him cringing, even though she didn't know what he looked like. "Well, yes."

"I've got plans today," she said, which felt like the truth to her, even though she didn't.

"You do?" His voice went high with surprise, then low again, forlorn. "Oh. Oh, well, is there a day that's better for you?"

"Stan, this is all kind of weird, you know," she finally said.

"Steve," he corrected. "And, I know. I'm sorry. I fail at this sort of thing. Look, just, don't say no now. Think it over and I'll call you again in a couple of days, okay? I'm sorry. I know I just made a terrible first impression, but...I'm sorry."

He hung up. Wren sat there staring at his number, wondering who had put weird pills in the campus water supply. It wasn't until she got back to her desk later that she realized she should have asked if he'd sent the flower.

* * * *

When she left work later, she found herself torn between dreading Steve calling again and hoping that Derek would, even though he might not be calling for the reason she hoped. It wasn't until after she'd eaten some frozen pizza and was on the treadmill zoning out, not watching flickering TV, that it occurred to her that after Abby was found, Derek wouldn't be in her employ anymore, and then there wouldn't be a conflict. Her heart skipped a beat literally—the monitor on the treadmill beeped—as she thought about it. But would he be as kind and caring and interested in her if she were just a face on the street? She had the feeling he really liked her, though....

Wren trusted her feelings. Usually.

That night, she had another erotic dream. It started out about Derek—big surprise, casting him in one of her typical dreams. Kissing, heat rising, hurrying from where they were, trying to find someplace private. She'd had this same dream about almost every guy she'd been at all attracted to since she was fourteen. Of course, it being a dream, the more and more and more they looked for a private place to have sex, the more outlandish the reasons such a place was unavailable. They were behind a movie theater, but there were people dancing in the parking lot, so they couldn't do it in the car. Derek tried to buy tickets to the movie inside, but then his wallet was stuck in his pocket and wouldn't come out, even with Wren tugging on it too. She eventually realized it was because his erection was too large, making his pants too tight and making her quake with both desire and fear. She paid with a credit card herself and they went into the theater, but could not go up to the balcony because the stairs were covered with ice, and several attempts to climb them failed. They decided to try the back row of the theater, but just as they reached the doors, the alien invaders in the film came to life and started eating the patrons.

She woke with her panties damp and her heart pounding, but too sleepy to actually touch herself. She slipped back into sleep.

The next dream found her waking in a pool of white light, lying on her back, surrounded by softness. Something silky caressed her skin and she arched up into the touch, but it was feather-light. She looked down to see the calla lily, held above her by a man's hand that seemed to come out of the white mist and brightness. He stroked her belly with it, as if drawing lines toward the center of her heat, the throbbing place between her legs. Her nipples stood under the caressing touch and she reached up to touch them herself, only to find her wrists bound by satin ribbons. She could move her hands, but only a few inches, and a soothing "shhhhh" came from above her.

The flower made its way lower, until at last it brushed between her thighs, encouraging her to spread her legs wider, wider, trying to get just a bit more stimulation in the right place. Her hips bucked, and a warm hand came down on her abdomen to hold her still.

A voice whispered. "Do you want pleasure?"

"Yes," Wren answered, also in a whisper. She didn't know the rules of this place, didn't know what might offend those who made them.

"You haven't said yes to pleasure, Wren," came the answer.

"I haven't?"

"No." Another feather-light brush of the flower sent a spark through her but it wasn't enough, wasn't nearly enough. "Don't be afraid."

"I'm not," she said, a little louder, but it didn't sound like the truth.

She woke with a shudder to sunlight in the windows but it was still another hour to go before her alarm would go off. She didn't want to wait. She climbed impatiently into the shower, thinking that she must have it really bad if her subconscious was talking to her that directly.

Chapter Three

WREN GOT to work late, not for any particular reason other than she'd ended up taking a long time in the shower, didn't want to hurry through breakfast, stopped to get gas on the way.

Oh, who was she kidding? She didn't want to run into Steve, if he was hanging around trying to catch her coming in. He sounded nice enough, he really did. But Wren didn't like pushy, even if it was his infatuation that had made a painfully shy guy into Mr. Pushy.

It didn't make sense, she thought. If he was so shy, that now he'd suddenly be reaching out to her. Maybe he had a therapist who encouraged him to do it? She hoped so. She didn't want to be the one to deal with it.

When she got to her desk, there was a new flower there. The same vase, but now it held a waxy red bloom with a single powdery stalk rising from the center. She blushed looking at it, remembering the vivid dream she'd woken to. No note again, of course.

Instead of getting right to work upon logging in, she opened a Web browser and searched for "red tropical flower," trying to find the name of the thing. It was fire-engine red, sort of heart-shaped—the more she looked at it, the more pornographic it seemed. "Anthurium," she murmured, after just a minute or two of searching yielded a picture. Well, they were common enough at florists', but she couldn't help but think the meaning was blatantly sexual.

Wren moved the vase to the side desk where she wouldn't see it and tried to concentrate on work, but after an hour, she found she was making mistakes due to inattention and she sighed. With a glance around, she opened up the Web browser again to check her e-mail. Technically it was not against the rules to check her non-work e-mail, but she always felt funny about doing it. It was lunchtime now, Wren rationalized, so it was okay, right?

She felt a little jolt go through her as she saw there was a message from Derek.

Had an interesting night last night and might be onto something. Give me a call when you can, or e-mail back. I'd rather tell you more in person, so let me know when you're free. I can drop by or we can meet.

Now she knew she wasn't going to get any more work done. She nearly fired back an e-mail to say "drop by for dinner and I'll order take-out" when she realized she'd just fidget all afternoon. Instead she sent a quick e-mail from her work account to library administration saying she was taking the rest of the day off, logged out, put her jacket back on, and picked up her purse. She left the flower where it was and walked quickly back to her car.

A tow truck was there, hoisting up a red van. Probably illegally parked. She got in her car but had to wait for the truck to clear. Might as well make a few phone calls.

She tried Abby's number again, and again got the message about the number temporarily out of service. Then she dialed Derek's number, but got his voice mail. Disappointment flooded through her. "Derek, it's Wren. I'm taking the rest of the day off, so any time you want to meet, I'm free. I'm out doing errands. Call me back."

Errands didn't seem like such a bad idea, anyway. She had been meaning to drop by the store and get a new toilet paper holder for weeks now, ever since accidentally breaking the previous one. Like a lot of things in the condo, it had looked nice but was cheap. Since then, she'd just been putting the roll on the back of the toilet and didn't really care. Whoever saw the bathroom off her bedroom but her?

But as she stood in the bathroom fixtures aisle looking at a dozen different styles of rollers, she had to admit to herself that she kind of hoped that maybe someone, someday, besides her, might see the bedroom.

Her phone ringing startled her. "White or brass?" she said, the moment she opened it.

Thank God, it was Derek and not Steve. "Excuse me?"

"No questions, just pick one."

"Um, brass."

"Okay." She tucked the brass fixture under her arm and started walking toward the cash registers, the phone crooked on her shoulder. "How are you?"

She thought she could hear him smiling through the phone. "Pretty good. I got your message. Will you be home in a while?"

"Yeah." Wren set her things down on the counter and the cashier rang up the purchase without ever making eye contact with her. "Want to come by for take-out? I'm thinking Chinese. Or maybe sushi. There's a place that delivers that now, too."

"Chinese is fine. Around six? Or sooner? We could talk first."

"Sooner," she found herself saying. "In fact, I haven't had lunch yet."

"Why don't you come by my office, then? You can park in the lot here and there's a new sushi place next door we could try."

"That sounds really good." She took a deep breath, wondering if it was her imagination, or if he really sounded as eager to see her as she thought. It was all supposedly about Abby, about the case, but it sounded—it felt—like flirting. No, not even flirting, like real interest.

Derek Chapman, she thought, *I'm falling in like with you.*

With a start, she realized the cashier was now glaring at her. She swiped her credit card quickly through the reader, signed on the pad, and hurried out. The phone started ringing again as she approached her car—Steve's number showed on the screen. She shoved the phone in her pocket. Maybe he'd leave a message.

* * * *

They sat at a table in one corner. The lunch rush was over and the restaurant was quiet except for the radio the sushi chef was playing and his occasional attempts to sing along with it.

One of the things about sushi, Wren found, is that everything came in orders of two, which made it very hard not to contemplate sharing things. Especially when Derek would eat something, get a rapturous look on his face, and then ask if she wanted to eat his other piece of whatever it was. "I'll trade it for a piece of your spicy tuna roll," he'd say.

One of the pieces he gave her was suspiciously white. "Is it real? It's whiter than tofu," she said, eyeing the little slice of fish on its oblong ball of rice.

"They call it white tuna," he said. "Apparently it's not really tuna, it's some other fish, but it's an actual fish. You haven't tried it before?"

She shook her head but picked it up, dipped the barest corner of it into her soy sauce, and popped it into her mouth.

The fish seemed to melt as she chewed it, better than any actual tuna she could remember tasting. She made a happy sound, then took a sip of salty miso soup to follow it. "That was good. Want a piece of my eel?" It was one of the things she saw he hadn't gotten. He made a slight face. "Oh, come on. I didn't try it for years because I thought eels were... weird. But they're just a long, skinny fish. And they make it really soft when they cook it."

"I always turned my nose up at the cooked part," he said, "but I'll try it."

She smiled as his face took on that blissful look again. "Told you it was good," she said.

She was enjoying herself and his company so much she almost forgot that he had something to tell her about Abby. *Had an interesting night last night,* he had written. What did that mean?

Wren supposed if it were urgent, he would have called her to tell her right away, or at the very least told her as soon as they sat down. But soon enough they were eating their dessert, balls of ice cream wrapped in a kind of cookie dough made from rice, and sipping their last refills of the green tea that tasted like roasted rice.

"So...I told you I'm working on this other missing persons case, right?" he said, leaning back with the teacup in his hand and glancing out the window. "The case has taken me to some pretty outlandish places. One of them is a kind of nightclub, a private club, and I was there last night. And the thing is...I thought I saw Abby there."

Wren waited for him to go on. He looked out the window again, and his cheeks had a slight blush to them.

"I couldn't get near enough to talk to her, and she disappeared into a section of the club where single men aren't allowed to go. I asked one of the other women who worked there, and she said she wasn't sure who I meant, didn't know her name, but I got the impression that the Abby lookalike worked there." He gave a little shrug.

"So, you could go back tonight and ask around for her again?" Wren asked.

"Well, they are only open three nights a week, and Sundays are the only nights they let new people in. Um, private club," he repeated. Now he was blushing full on.

Wren set her teacup down. "What do you mean private club? Like a strip club? It wouldn't surprise me at all if Abby became a stripper, you know."

He smiled a little then, but still didn't meet her eyes. "Not a strip club," he said. "It's a...kind of couples' club. That's why as a single man I couldn't go beyond the lounge."

"Couples' club?" As she said it though, his blushing came to make sense. "I suppose they aren't getting together to play bridge. Is that what you're saying?"

He nodded gratefully. "I plan to go back next week, with... with a female friend who's also a private investigator. She... she specializes in cheating husbands so she's been there before. They really, really don't like people asking questions. The whole thing is kind of not wholly legal. Well, I mean the sex is. There's no law against couples having sex with each other at a...a party if they want to. But as a business, they don't have regular employee records, for example. And of course, their member list is highly secret...."

He ground to a halt and gave her a concerned look. "It'll be all right, Wren."

Wren realized she was frowning at him. "You and this friend, it's strictly business?"

She was gratified to see the stricken look that fell over him now. "Strictly! Very." It took him a moment to gather his wits and a full sentence. "Diana and I share that office. We've worked together a lot. She's not only married, she's fifteen years older than me. If it'd make you feel better, you could meet her."

Wren wrapped her hands around the teacup, a pang of guilt going through her for making him defend himself. It wasn't as if she really had any right to be jealous, did she? But he reacted as if she did.

She wanted to say the words. *Derek, do you like me?* But she held her tongue. That was so junior high school. And it was obvious he liked her, wasn't it?

"Okay," she said instead. Then she remembered. "Are we still on for dinner, too?"

"If you like," he said softly, his voice a little tentative. "I'd like that."

Oh, Jesus, now he's feeling insecure because I scolded him.

It was kind of cute.

"You're not backing out, are you?" she teased.

"No! Just checking."

He insisted on paying for lunch, saying she could cover dinner if they still wanted to keep things even.

* * * *

It wasn't until after she'd followed him all the way to his car at eleven that night to say goodbye to him that she realized she just didn't want him to go. She wanted him to kiss her goodnight, but that would have been way too obviously wrong, too much beyond the plausible state of friendship they had now. It was okay to be friendly and still have a business relationship, apparently, but kisses good night were right out. She stood in the driveway watching him back out, and he waved from the street as he put his car in gear and then drove off.

The condo seemed very empty and quiet after the hours and hours she and Derek had spent talking.

She'd dragged out her old photo albums, ostensibly to show him all the pictures of Abby so maybe he'd recognize her better next time, but she ended up showing him all of them, even all her baby pictures and childhood photos of trips to the beach, amusement parks, and Christmas at various relatives' houses.

Wren sighed. She wasn't going to see him again until—when? It was a whole week until he could look for Abby again.

She tried to put it out of her mind. She would see him when she'd see him, and maybe in the meantime she could e-mail him some jokes or something.

* * * *

The next morning, her mind was still on him when she arrived at work. The flowers had slipped her mind completely until she got to her desk and there was another one. This one was a sprig of mountain laurel, each spray of tiny, white bell-shaped blossoms hanging like a tassel. The scent was lovely.

Pretending Derek had sent it, Wren decided she'd just ignore Steve if he called. He hadn't left a message. She sent Derek a recycled joke e-mail in the mid-afternoon, but hadn't heard back from him by four-thirty when she left work. It didn't even look as if Steve had tried to call this time, which was a relief.

At home, she did forty-five minutes on the treadmill, installed the new toilet paper roller, and ended up thoroughly cleaning the bathroom, including taking everything out of the medicine cabinet, cleaning all the shelves in it, and throwing away at least a third of the stuff in there that was old or expired. She didn't even realize how late it was getting until her stomach grumbled. She ate a bowl of microwaved macaroni and cheese, then got in bed with a book.

Before she'd read five pages, she was asleep.

Of course there were dreams, but the dreams didn't turn lucid, didn't turn erotic, until later. When it did, Wren found herself in the basement room that was starting to seem familiar. She could see the painted cinderblock, the pattern muted by multiple layers of paint.

"Put your hands over your head."

The voice came just in her ear and she jumped. She was standing with her hands bound in front of her. She raised them, exposing her breasts, and her breath caught. Someone off to the side tugged at the bindings and she found herself affixed to the wall. Hung like a picture frame. A bright light shone down on her from the ceiling, making her blink. Beyond the bright cone, she could see nothing in the darkness.

Then a hand reached into the light, twirling the spray of mountain laurel in its fingers. *His fingers,* she thought. It was definitely a man's hand.

"Lovely," said the voice from the darkness, as the hand painted air across her stomach with the flowers, using the tassel-like chains of the blossoms as a brush. Then again, and again, swinging the flowers gently in a crisscross until the skin all over her stomach and breasts tingled from this strange scourging. Her nipples stood up eagerly, as if trying to catch the brush on each pass.

"Spread your feet apart."

She did as she was told, her arms above her pulled taut, though she wondered, *what would happen if she said no?* She was lucid, quite clear that she was dreaming, and she wondered if she could exert her will, her desire, on this dreamscape.

Cool air on hot flesh, and then the cool brush of the flowers, upward and upward and upward, until she was panting and crying, wanting more, needing more, inflamed and aroused, yet she would never reach climax this way.

"Please," she said, forming her lips around the word, forcing the sound out, as if fighting against the dream. "Please, I need..." Dream logic said if her dream partner made her come, she wouldn't have to do it herself when she woke.

And please let it be Derek there in the dark, she thought. Why did her mind have to wrap everything up in symbols and metaphors? Why couldn't she just have a nice, normal fantasy about the attractive man she knew?

She tried to imagine him stepping into the light, nude, looking like a Greek statue, his cock in a nest of curls as dark as the hair on his head. He'd wrap his arms around her, rubbing his crotch against her leg until he was so hot and hard he needed to quench the fire in the wet depths of her.

"Derek..." she whispered, and her heart stuttered as the motion of the flower ceased. She blinked as the hand was withdrawn into the darkness. Was he about to step into the light as she imagined?

No, no, it was too early for the dream to be over, wasn't it? The light seemed to be muting but she suddenly realized she was lying on her back, staring up at the white ceiling above the bed. A sunbeam had just strayed past her pillow— it must have been shining on her eyelids and that was where the bright light in the dream came from. Of course the flower came from today's "secret admirer" on her mind. Though how it was used—she'd certainly never done or even thought of anything like that before.

She groaned and insinuated a finger between her slick folds.

* * * *

By Thursday, she was restless and irritable. She had even snapped at Steve the one time she'd answered the phone and felt guilty immediately after hanging up. The poor guy was probably never going to have the guts to talk to another woman again. The flowers stopped appearing on her desk, though they continued to appear in her dreams.

She ended up calling Steve back to apologize and learned something that made her worry that maybe encouraging him wasn't such a good idea.

"I have an apology to make, too," he'd said. "Er, you might not remember it now, but you got a random call from a stranger claiming to be calling a personal ad?"

"Of course I remember that," she said, irked anew.

"Yeah, well, um, that was me. My first attempt at trying to talk to you. It was so stupid. I'm so sorry. You've been so nice to me."

She felt guiltier because she wasn't being nice at all. She hung up on him again.

Meanwhile, Derek and she had kept up a steady stream of little e-mails to each other, two or three a day of jokes, funny pictures of cats, and amusing news stories. When she saw one from him on Thursday afternoon, she opened it expecting nothing of consequence. But along with the cartoon, he'd sent a note saying, "Diana has a conflict. Can we talk about the plan for the weekend?"

She couldn't help but be amused. To anyone else who might read her e-mail it might appear she had a boyfriend and this was just about making social plans with friends. Instead, she called him from her car on her way home.

"Diana's got a family emergency," he told her, while she was stopped at a red light. "She has to fly home. Her mother's in the hospital."

"Oh," Wren said.

"I had an idea, though. Can I come over to tell you?"

She took her foot off the brake as the light changed. "Um, sure."

"You don't sound so sure."

Was she hesitant to see him? It was just hard having to maintain a distance. "Just distracted. I'm driving."

He made a scolding noise. "I'll be there in a little while, okay?"

She stuffed the phone back into her purse and looked around guiltily. Okay, so she shouldn't be trying to talk on the phone and drive. It just went to show how nuts she was for him.

He pulled up about twenty minutes later. She'd chit-chatted with Lawrence a bit and had just changed her clothes when he rang the bell.

"Have you had dinner yet?" she asked, the moment he was in the door.

"Er, no, but I didn't intend..."

She waved her hand until he trailed off. "It's okay. I don't mind making a habit of this. I was just going to boil some pasta. I can do it as easily for two as one." And she was really tired of eating alone.

"All right." He gave in easily and she wondered if maybe he was tired of eating alone, too.

She started filling a pot with water, and he dug some vegetables out of the crisper for salad. They worked without speaking for a little while, and she started sautéing some garlic and mushrooms in a saucepan, then added the jar sauce she liked.

"Did Diana say what's wrong with her mother?" she asked, when the noodles had gone into the water.

Derek set the salad on the table. "She didn't know. Possibly a stroke. They weren't sure at the time when she collapsed, and Diana went off to the airport before I heard anything more. I guess she's been having health problems for a while, so this wasn't totally unexpected, but..." He shrugged. "I'm not sure if she doesn't want to talk about it, or if she's uncomfortable talking about it with me in particular."

Wren nodded and resisted the urge to stir the pasta. "So is the trip to the club on Sunday off completely, then?"

"Assuming she doesn't get back in time, which seems likely. Well." He leaned against one of the stools without completely sitting on it. "I did have another idea."

Wren waited for him to go on. She knew this was where she was supposed to say, "what?" but she never liked feeling like a dog who barks when trained to. If he was going to tell her anyway, why should she have to prod him?

He met her eyes and didn't speak for a few seconds. Then, "You could come with me. In fact, I had wanted to ask you to do it in the first place, since you'd be the most likely to recognize your sister anyway. But I didn't want to put you in an embarrassing position. Or make you do anything you wouldn't be comfortable doing."

She took a deep breath. "What would we have to do?"

He was blushing and it was cute, even if what they were talking about was serious. "We'd be acting like a couple, so I guess, like, holding hands and acting affectionate, and like it was really exciting for us to be there. There are rooms deeper in where only couples can go. Since we'd be new, we could act curious and ask questions that probably a single man couldn't. They're very suspicious of single guys."

Wren snorted. "Because single guys might be only interested in sex? It's a sex club. That doesn't make much sense."

Derek put his hands up. "I have no idea. Maybe too many husbands get jealous."

The timer beeped and she drained the pasta, then put it back in the pot and tossed it with the sauce, shaking grated cheese over the whole thing, only remembering to ask, "Um, grated cheese okay?" after it was too late.

"Sure," he said with a laugh as they moved to the table. "Seriously, Wren, you can say no and I'll just wait until Diana gets back."

"It sounds kind of intriguing," she said, as she picked up her fork. "I mean, when else would I get a chance to see inside a place like that? If we don't like it, we can just leave, right? I mean, if we were a married couple checking it out or something. Surely there are people who go there and decide it's not for them."

"True." He still looked a little worried, though. "We'd have to...dress up."

Wren stopped with her fork halfway to her mouth. "In what?"

"Well, I can get away with a pair of leather pants and no shirt. And some of the women I saw didn't, uh, didn't wear anything, really, just a thong maybe. But, so yeah, you'd probably want some kind of lingerie to wear or something like that."

He was almost stammering by the end of his sentence and Wren found herself grinning. Cute. "Some kind of lingerie," she repeated. "I've got a couple of old slips but I doubt they'd work." She thought for a minute. "How out there is the stuff the women wear? Like would something nice but opaque from Victoria's Secret be all right?"

"I'd think so," he said. "I'd guess that any young couple just joining this club would ask these same questions, and probably come up with the same answers."

She nodded. "I'll go shopping tomorrow after work. I'm sure I can come up with something that'll be okay."

"You're sure? You're really sure?"

She resisted the urge to grab him by the hand. "I'm sure. It'll be an adventure, right? We'll probably find Abby and she'll chew me out for being there, but at least I'll know she's okay, and then it will all be over with."

* * * *

After Derek left, she sent Lawrence an e-mail asking if he wanted to go shopping the next night. She would have just called him on the phone or knocked on his door, but she wasn't ready to explain the errand they would be doing just yet.

When she got home on Friday night, Lawrence was waiting for her, and as they got into her car he asked, "So what are we shopping for? Or did you just want company while getting a head start on Christmas?"

She kept both hands on the wheel and her eyes on the road as she answered, completely and truthfully, "I want your help picking out some clothes."

Lawrence laughed. "And you figured your gay friend would have an eye and taste? We're not all fashion geniuses, you know."

She clucked her tongue. "No, but you are. And I need the moral support." *Damn, shouldn't have said that,* she thought. The comment made him suspicious.

"Why, are you planning to buy something horribly expensive?"

"Well, I hope not...."

"Oh, God, Wren, you're not starting wedding dress shopping or something like that?"

She snorted, thinking it was actually the opposite. "Hardly."

"You mean you're not serious about that good-looking guy you introduced me to? Daniel?"

"Derek," she corrected. "And okay, yeah, I really like him, but I hired him to find Abby. He's a detective." Was that the right word? Maybe for Lawrence it was. "He thinks maybe he saw her recently, and now I'm going to go with him to see if I can identify her."

Lawrence took all that in without interrupting. "It's not all an excuse to get you out on a date? What sort of a place is he taking you?"

"A club," she said, and left it at that, her eyes on the road.

"And you need clothes." Lawrence nodded with understanding, even if he was wrong about what kind of club. "You want to pick something that will flatter you and look nice, so that when you find your sister, then you can ask him out?"

Wren pulled the car into the parking lot of the mall. "Yes. Yes, that sounds like a good idea, anyway. Now help me look for a parking space."

Once they were inside the mall, Lawrence didn't suspect a thing until they went to the second floor and Wren refused to go into the store he tried to drag her into, instead insisting she had a place in mind. She half-dragged him on a beeline for Victoria's Secret.

"Wren, I know what girls wear to clubs these days is skimpy, but...."

"Hush up," she said, pulling him up to the window, but not going in just yet. "The part I didn't tell you is that *maybe* the reason Abby hasn't contacted me is because she's working at this...this couples' club."

"You mean a *swingers* club?" Lawrence's voice dropped to a scandalized whisper.

Wren grimaced. "I guess so? It's some place where couples go to, like, be exhibitionists, I guess."

Lawrence wrinkled his nose. "And he wants you to go there with him? Wren, that sounds like a set-up to me."

"Lawrence!" She made an exasperated noise. "I hired him, remember?"

"Have you really thought about it? I mean, a sex club? What if some creepy guy asks to have sex with you? Or some creepy woman, for that matter?" He squeezed her hand urgently.

"I'll tell them I'm not interested, right? Derek will protect me, too. It's not like I'm wandering in there alone and drunk or something."

"You know about roofies, right? The date rape drug? You could both end up on skeevy videos on the Internet and like, violated." He shuddered with revulsion.

"Stop being so dramatic. We're going to go in, look around, and maybe ask around for her, and leave. But we have to look like we want to be there." She squeezed his hand back. "I'm betting it won't be half as exciting as we're making it out to be, anyway. A place for married couples who have gotten so bored they need to go out and do it in front of people because that's the only way it can be exciting anymore?"

Lawrence took a handkerchief out of his pocket and patted his forehead. "All right. Well, let's go in."

They went in together and Wren found herself putting a hand through the crook of his arm. She steered him toward what looked like a safe place to start, a rack of hats. She wasn't going to wear one, probably, but at least it got them started. She pulled one onto her head and looked at herself in the mirror. Lawrence huffed, took it off her and replaced it with another one, then another one. "Your new haircut looks too good to hide it under a hat," he declared, setting the final hat aside.

Wren giggled as his fingers tickled the back of her neck. "Quit that!"

He pulled his hand back. "Sorry! It's just, did you know you have a heart-shaped birthmark under your hair? You would never be able to see it when you had more hair."

"Really?" She turned and tried to see in the mirror, but it was on the back of her head where she had no chance to see it.

"Yeah. about the size of a dime, and not very dark. It's cute," Lawrence said. "Now, you didn't come in here to look at hats."

"You're right." She headed toward a rack of camisoles that were all yellow and burnt umber. She took one off the rack and held it up.

He shook his head. "You're a winter. Your skin is bluish so if you wear anything with yellow in it you will look seasick green."

"So what should I look for?"

"Blue or black. Maybe forest green? Maybe. Although it doesn't look like that color is in." He raised a hand to his brow like a ranger shading his eyes on the Serengeti while he looked for wildlife. "Ugh, I hate fall. It's all earth tones. They are all wrong for you."

"You should see this place in the winter," Wren said, a bit sullenly. "All red and pink because of Valentine's Day. I avoid it like crazy. Not that I really have ever shopped here."

She looked back and forth conspiratorially. "They always look at me like I'm somehow beneath them. The salesgirls, I mean."

Lawrence continued his scanning and then pulled her slowly toward some long, satin robes. "They have been eyeing us with a kind of belligerent disinterest since we came in," he added, as he ran his fingers down the cloth. "Something like this would be perfect if it weren't brown or any variation thereof." They drifted through the store a bit more. "There's not a single thing in here that's black except that one little pile of panties on the table. That's so strange. I always thought it was one of lingerie's standard colors."

Wren shrugged. "Maybe they think it's too trashy-looking? Maybe we should have gone to Frederick's of Hollywood instead? There's one of those in the West Center Mall."

Lawrence made a face like he'd tasted something that had gone bad. "Perhaps we'd be better off to try the lingerie department in the department store. There's not a single thing in here that's blue, either." He looked at her seriously. "Why should you spend your money in a place where they aren't nice to you? These bitches don't know shit."

That made Wren laugh, which only seemed to attract more suppressed ire from the salesgirls, though she wasn't sure if it was his suddenly colorful language or her laughing that did it. Probably her laughing, since she doubted—hoped—no one had heard Lawrence's comment but her. She held his hand as they left the store, head high.

Chapter Four

TWO NIGHTS later she stood just inside the building, watching through the high window in the door for Derek's car. She clutched the handle of her overnight bag in both hands. They'd be changing clothes there. It was one of the rules of the club that everyone went in looking "normal" and came out again the same way. The sun had set, but there was still golden light in the sky as his SUV pulled into the driveway and she hurried down the steps to meet him.

She climbed into the passenger seat and shut the door. "Um, hi."

"Hi." He smiled. "Ready to go? Wait, forget that, stupid question. How are you?"

She answered with some pat answer, and he didn't press, as they drove along the river to the other side of town. They were both silent as they went, and when Wren guessed they were getting close to their destination, she cleared her throat.

"I'm a little nervous," she admitted. "Do you want to know the truth?"

He glanced at her as he turned into a parking lot. "Do I?"

She bit her lip. *I hope you do.* "I really wish...we were going somewhere together for the sake of going somewhere together. Not for the case."

"That's a very good wish," he said softly as he brought the car to a stop. "I wish that, too."

Wren swallowed, trying to keep her heart in her chest. "Oh, good." His smile seemed to soothe her. Neither of them seemed to know what to say after that, so she opened her door and got out.

They were standing outside a low brick building in the parking lot where another building had once stood. They went around to the front and it seemed to Wren that there were no windows. There was no sign, either, just fairly fresh-looking black paint on the bricks, and two potted evergreens, each five feet tall, one on each side of the doorway. Derek pulled open the door and they entered a dimly lit entrance room with a girl at a cash register, an unmanned coat check stand across from her. Everything was draped in heavy cloth, like backstage curtains. Derek gave his name and Wren was surprised he used his real name. The girl asked to see their IDs but it looked like it was just to verify their ages, and she crossed Derek off of a list. Wren was also surprised that no money exchanged hands. The girl pointed to the double doors that led further in, and reminded Derek that the changing rooms were to the left after entering. "Have a good time!"

There were separate rooms for the men and the women to change clothes in. She wasn't sure why that should be surprising, but it struck her as funny that a place where everyone went to get a look at each other's yayas would feel the need to separate the changing rooms. Not that she wasn't grateful for it. She didn't want Derek watching her figure out how to get her outfit on.

In the end, she and Lawrence had settled on a midnight blue so dark it would look black under most light. It was a halter-top chemise that came to mid-thigh, with a matching short robe of the same length, and matching panties that she hoped no one was going to see anyway, but they came with the set. She would have loved if pajama bottoms also came in the set, but they did not, and she really didn't think she'd be comfortable in stockings, so she planned to go bare-legged. A pair of satin ballet-style slip-ons completed the outfit.

She looked in the mirror. Her eyeshadow and liner were dark blue to match as well, and she was surprised at how glamorous she looked, like a black and white photograph from some French fashion magazine, just a tinge of color added. The chemise could almost be an evening dress, if she were wearing pearls. The satin moved like water over her skin, feeling so light it felt as if all she was wearing was a caress. She had to keep looking down to be sure she was still covered.

She was just turning to put her normal clothes away when another woman came in. She had frizzy red hair and sat down heavily on the chair in front of the lockers. "Oh good," she said to Wren when she saw her. "Could you help me get into my corset?"

"Um...."

The woman laughed. She looked to be in her mid-forties, rather heavyset. "It's not as tough as it sounds. I just need someone to hold the laces for me. It's impossible to do it alone. I'm Suzanne." She held out a meaty hand, and Wren shook it. Suzanne's wedding ring and engagement ring shone on the other hand as she pulled herself up out of the chair. "Your first time here?"

"Um, yes," Wren said and waited to be told what to do.

"My second," Suzanne said, as she put her glasses into a locker and began pulling her sweater off. "Although my husband and I used to go to swingers conventions all the time. Malibu Beach, Las Vegas, the Caribbean—we used to go like two or three times a year. But we're becoming more home-bodies now that we're getting older, and right now money's tight. This place seems all right, though, so far."

"Does it?" Wren asked, without meaning for it to come out as tentative as it did.

Suzanne laughed again. "Yeah. Seems clean, and they keep the pervs out. Well, the bad pervs, I mean. I heard on the news, some place in Texas, a swingers club where the guy drugged his ten-year-old niece and nephew every night and made them perform sex acts on stage. That kind of stuff is just sick, sick, sick."

"Oh, God." Wren sat on the bench next to the lockers. "Jesus."

"Yeah, makes you think, who the hell is sick enough to even go to a place like that? But that's the thing. Only people already so ashamed of what they are doing would keep their mouths shut. It didn't take long for someone with some common sense to call the cops. There's nothing wrong with some consenting couples getting together for a little fun, or even a lot of fun. The more accepting people are of that, the less crap like that will happen. Anyway, as I was saying, this place doesn't seem like that. They're real careful, there's no drugs allowed at all, and even the drinks they serve are watered down."

She turned to Wren now dressed in leather boots up to mid-thigh, with a gold and red brocade corset wrapped around her waist. She was hooking the two front flaps together where they had little hook-and-eyes.

In the back was a crisscross of laces, coming together in a loose bow right at the center of her back. She turned around again and pointed to the bow. "All you have to do is untie that, pull tight, and then tie it like you tie a sneaker. Okay?"

"Okay," Wren said, and put her hands against the ribs of the corset for a second just to feel what it was like. Very hard, almost like a shell or armor. She pulled on the laces.

"A little more," Suzanne said with a laugh. "I can still breathe."

Wren giggled. "All right." She pulled hard this time, and then tied the knot like she would on a birthday gift that was trying to come undone.

"Perfect!" Suzanne declared, adjusting the lie of her ample bosom in the top of the garment. "Now let's go, or the menfolk will think we started having fun by ourselves. I'll introduce you to my husband, Bob. What was your name again?"

"Wren."

"Ren? Is that short for something?"

"Um, no, like the bird."

"Oh, okay. You'll find some people don't use their real names in the swinging scene, but Bob and I kept forgetting what names to use." She pushed open a different door than the one Wren had entered through, and led her into a lounge area. A bartender was working in one corner, and music was playing, but not too loud. "People would be like 'Hi, Kim!'

or whatever and I'd be like...is she talking to me? So we just stick with Bob and Suzanne."

Wren was introduced to Bob, who seemed friendly without being too friendly. He was going bald, had a paunch, and was wearing a Hawaiian shirt with bikini bathing beauties all over it and loose surfer-style shorts. Wren looked around for Derek but didn't see him.

"Young guy, tall and skinny, black hair? Oh, he's in there, still," Bob said. "He got a call on his cell phone and went into the head to take it."

"Oh, okay," Wren said. She didn't think of Derek as skinny, but maybe Bob did.

Suzanne suggested they get drinks, and Wren was just starting to wonder how people paid for things, if there was nowhere to carry a wallet in lingerie. But just then Derek emerged. As he'd promised, he was wearing a pair of leather pants and nothing else. Even his feet were bare, and that suddenly struck Wren as even more decadent than wearing boots like Suzanne. Like he'd just come from strolling up the white sand of a deserted Caribbean beach. She wondered if that was how Bob looked to Suzanne in his surfer shorts?

"Hey, beautiful," Derek said, and slipped his hands around her waist and gave her a peck on the cheek.

Right. They were supposed to look like a young couple out for some adventure. "Hey," she said back, and went up on tiptoe to kiss him just in front of his ear. The scent of leather and just a hint of his soap, and what had to be his skin, sent a shiver through her. "Um, this is Suzanne and Bob. They've been kind of teaching me the ropes."

Bob guffawed. "Naw, we'd have to go to another kind of club for ropes." He held out his hand and shook Derek's.

Within a few minutes, everyone had drinks in hand and Derek was pumping the couple for information. It was easy to do: they clearly enjoyed telling tales of the swingers' circuit and helping out the "newbies." Bob described the setup here, how it was different from some other places; how here, there was a series of rooms, and depending on how far you wanted to go or what you were willing to do, you went further and further in. Wren looked around at the other couples, wondering how deep each of them would go. Most of them shared a drink or two, chatted a little with the others, and then would pass through a door painted silver, a design of a vine with heart-shaped leaves in darker silver painted over that.

But then everyone's drinks were empty. Wren hadn't even realized she'd finished her Blue Hawaiian, but she put the glass down on the tray by the bar with the others.

"Well, you all have a good time," Suzanne said to them. "We're going to go on and check out the next room."

Derek held out a hand for Wren. "I suppose we should do the same. Ready?"

Wren just nodded, thankful that she hadn't tried to wear high heels. The rum was going straight to her head. She took his hand and they went through the silver door, following the hearty sound of Suzanne's laughter.

* * * *

The door led into a hallway, as it turned out, carpeted with a nice Oriental rug, with an ornate lamp sitting on a wooden side table, like you'd find in the hall of an old hotel. They went through another silver door on the right, and into a room with a soft pinkish light and subtly pulsing music.

The vine design painted on it was larger than the one on the previous door, Wren noticed, with more leaves.

There were about a dozen people here, along with two single women whom Wren eventually decided must be employees. They were both in high heels with similar corsets and short, sheer ruffled skirts, through which Wren could see their dark panties, even in the dim light.

Some of the couples sat on couches and banquettes built into the wall. Everything was draped with sheets, and Wren tried not to stare at the couple closest to them, the woman in the man's lap and his hand between her legs. The sound of a woman sighing softly to her right caught her attention, and there a man sat with his back to the wall and his legs spread, his partner sitting between them and her legs spread also, his hand moving up and down under the sheer lace triangle of her panties. His attention was on his partner, as he kissed her neck and whispered softly to her, but the woman looked up, saw Wren looking, and smiled a dreamy smile.

Wren clutched Derek's elbow. She barely listened when one of the female employees came over and welcomed him and reminded him this was the foreplay room. Mutual masturbation was as far as people went in here, apparently, and—as Bob added after the woman had left—it was considered bad form for a single man to come in here, though for some reason women were okay.

"And it looks like we're just in time for the show." He and Suzanne took a seat just a few feet from the spread-legged couple Wren kept looking back at, and Derek urged her to sit next to him on Suzanne's other side.

The lights brightened at the other end of the room, and a small stage with a brass pole on it was illuminated. The music changed and got louder, and a burlesque dancer stepped up onto the platform.

She proceeded to do all manner of suggestive and acrobatic things with the pole, although Wren kept finding her eyes straying to the couples around her. One pair were kissing deeply, and then the man picked his partner up and carried her into the next room, where actual penetrative sex was allowed. One of the women took away the sheet they had been sitting on, like a waitress changing a tablecloth.

Wren found herself blushing and hoped the red tinge of the light hid it. She heard Suzanne giggle and looked up to see Bob had worked one of her breasts free of the corset and was sucking on it like a little baby, complete with num-num-num noises. They were clearly having fun. In particular, Wren noticed, all the women seemed so happy. Even the ones like Suzanne, who didn't look like porn models. They all seemed to feel sexy and beautiful.

She shivered, as Derek absently ran a hand up her arm. His eyes were on the dancer, sometimes glancing back to the door the woman had come through.

Wren put a hand on his shoulder, then leaned closer to whisper in his ear. "You should...you should kiss me. Um. So we'll fit in." God, his scent...

He turned his head so that their foreheads touched. "Wren..." But if he'd planned to say more, he didn't manage it before his lips touched hers.

Upon closing her eyes, she lost track of her hands as her entire world centered on the gentle nibble of his mouth, the fleeting sweep of his tongue. She tilted her head back further, her lips parting, and his tongue darted to touch hers. Something flared, hot and bright, desire igniting in her belly, thoughts flashing through her mind, like how good that same touch would feel on other parts of her, if only she dared...

Wren imagined him spreading her legs right here, running his fingers up and down the now-damp edge of her panties until he slipped a finger under the elastic, Suzanne and Bob watching. She could almost hear his voice as he'd whisper in her ear, like the other couple had been doing. *Wren, you're so beautiful,* he'd say. *I can't stop touching you. I want to show everyone you're beautiful and you're mine and this is the pleasure I can give you.*

To her dismay, he pulled back. "I don't...think we should go beyond this room," he whispered in her ear. "I think Abby was one of the women in here. Let's stay here as long as we can and see if we see her?"

"All right." Wren's hand slid along his jaw and she swallowed hard. Going into the other room meant having sex. Or breaking the rules by not doing it—no one was allowed to "just watch." It was, they said, part of how they kept the voyeurs out. "But if we're going to stay, you...you..."

He tilted her chin so he could look into her eyes. "If it's too much, we could..."

"You have to kiss me again." And she took a ragged breath as she waited for him to do so. This time he pulled her in, just with those two fingers under her chin, so she pressed against him as he leaned slightly back and brought her mouth to his.

This time his tongue met hers repeatedly, in a soft, relentless rhythm her body recognized and responded to before her mind did, her hips answering with a beat of their own against him. She groaned quietly, thinking, *oh God, I want him to touch me. Derek, please, oh please.*

His warm hand slipped around the curve of her buttock. They were sliding and moving and she almost didn't realize it, until he was flat on his back, pulling her astride him, grinding her pubic bone against the matching hardness under his zipper.

Wren had never wanted someone so much, not even in her fantasies. *Oh God, Derek, touch me, please touch me.*

He gripped her buttocks with both hands, then slid one around her thigh further, pulling aside the crotch of her panties and smearing his fingers in the ample wetness there. He slid them back and forth, back and forth, gradually parting her labia and exposing her clit to the same gentle treatment.

She cried out softly as the pads of his fingers brushed across it. *Oh, yes, yes, that's perfect.*

Wren, lovely Wren. I shouldn't have brought you here. But I'm not sorry I did. Not now.

The whispers only sent her desire soaring. *I've wanted you since I first saw you,* she thought. *I never dreamed it could feel like this.* She sank into the sensation, his fingers pushing her higher and higher, as quickly and surely as if she were doing it herself.

May I make you come? Please say yes.

Yes, oh yes...

She cried out against his shoulder, as spasms of pleasure wracked her body, as he trailed off the touch and sensation only gradually, still holding her close with the other hand, and then running it over her close-shorn hair. "God, you're beautiful...."

It was only when he spoke she realized with a jolt that he hadn't been speaking aloud before. She jerked upright and stared into his eyes. *Can you hear me?*

Derek blinked. *Yes. And you hear me?*

Yes. She swallowed, a sudden chill and goosebumps climbing up her back. *Oh my God.*

He reached up and brushed a finger across her lips. They tingled and she heard the thought under that: *My God, I've never seen anything so beautiful in all my life.* Then a more direct thought: *Can you hear anyone else?*

She looked up. Suzanne and Bob were gone and the dancer had finished. There was another couple in their place, the woman running her hand up and down the man's crotch. Then he unbuttoned his jeans and she pulled his pecker out, yanking on it.

Maybe. I think the guy next to us just wondered why she always squeezes his dick so hard. Wren found herself giggling. *But maybe I think that from the expression on his face. He's like: 'I shouldn't be ungrateful that she'll do this for me, but....'*

Derek laughed quietly. *What about the workers?*

She tried to concentrate on the woman changing the sheets on the couch across from them, but Wren's head was swimming too much. The air seemed close now, heavy with pheromones, and there was the rum and the orgasm and... she swayed and felt his hands holding her. "Can't..." she said, shaking her head.

"Okay," he whispered, and shifted their position until she was in his lap.

She tried once more to reach out as one of the women came close. She closed her eyes. She felt a sensation of sinking, like the feeling of falling asleep, except she was still awake.

When she opened her eyes, she was under the cone of light, her hands bound over her head. Her breath caught. Maybe she had fallen asleep then, and straight into a dream?

She could feel the wetness on her thighs, as if in the dream she had come directly from Derek's arms.

"Ahhhh," said a voice, just a whisper, off to one side. She felt a hand reach between her legs, rough fingers pushing her lips apart and smearing her juices back and forth. "So ripe, so ready."

She shook her head in alarm. "No, no I'm not ready at all."

"What did I say to you? Entry. Penetration. And it doesn't matter what part of me enters what part of you. Once I'm inside, I'm inside."

She gasped as two fingers were pushed inside her, a callused thumb rubbing her clit. "I guarantee you, my cock will feel better than this. And you'll enjoy it here more than any of your other holes."

The hand began to move and Wren cried out, thinking he was right. She wanted to be filled so very much right now. But not by her dream lover. By Derek. Wait, hadn't she decided Derek *was* her dream lover? But it didn't feel like him. Maybe the dream was just an expression of everything she feared but wanted at the same time.

"Ask me to take you, and I will," said the voice.

She shook her head, and then moaned in disappointment as the fingers were withdrawn.

"Hush, it's all right. You're just not ready yet. It's all right. I'll wait." Something soft touched her cheek and she turned her head into the heady scent of a rose.

The hand reaching out of the darkness held a perfect rose so red its veins were almost blue. The soft blossom trailed down her body, brushed upward at the folds between her legs. She moaned again, then gasped as the prick of one of the thorns scraped over her clit. She bit her lip as the point pressed in, not hard enough to pierce, but the sharpness of the prick made every hair stand on end, and her hips moved shamelessly, her flesh craving a more soothing stroke.

None came. The stem was pressed between her legs, and then the hands urged her knees together, until she was holding the thorns in place herself, hips still pumping as the light faded and left her in darkness.

* * * *

Somewhere beyond the rushing in her ears she could hear voices arguing, insistence and apology ringing and twining in the tones of the voices, a woman, a man, then nothing again.

When she woke properly, she felt cool air on her face and a jostling. Derek was carrying her to the car. He pressed a kiss to her forehead and then settled her in the passenger seat while the woman who followed behind them asked, "Are you sure she'll be all right?"

"I'll be fine," Wren said in a weak but audible voice. She wondered what Derek had told her. She waved a hand vaguely. "So sorry about that. I was having a lovely time."

The woman was different from the ones she had seen in the foreplay room; she was dressed in a track suit and looked more like a soccer mom than a sex club queen. The woman nodded and rubbed her own upper arms against the chill. "Please come back and see us again."

"We will," Derek said, and they waved to each other. He got in his side and started the engine. "Are you all right?"

Wren took a deep breath. "I don't know. That's...never happened before."

"Let's at least get you some water and a Tylenol," he said and backed out of the lot. "We're not far from my place. They gave me your clothes."

"That sounds good," Wren said, suddenly exhausted. She hadn't realized until he mentioned it that she was wrapped in her coat but still wearing the lingerie under it. What the hell had happened there? She tried to think about what happened without thinking about the dream, but she couldn't seem to escape the images—the sensations—that made her squirm in her seat. She could still feel the fingers probing her, the thorns pricking her... She stifled a little moan.

"Almost there," he said, and she wondered if he thought she were in pain.

He pulled into the garage of a small house, the light coming on automatically as the door went up, then closed behind them. Before Wren had quite realized it, he had come around to her side of the car and was helping her out. "I can walk." she said, but he had only just gotten the door into the house open when she sagged against him.

He picked her up again and carried her inside, setting her down somewhere soft and dark and helping her out of her coat. "Does your head hurt?" he asked in a quiet voice, his hands moving cool and smooth over her forehead as he lay back.

She kept her eyes closed. "No, don't think so. I had a dream...."

His weight settled next to hers. "What do you mean?"

"We were talking, you and I, mind-talking," she said, recalling it. "And then I had this feeling like I was falling. Almost like falling asleep, but not quite...but I fell into a dream that I've been having a lot lately." She felt her cheeks heat up.

"Hm. To me it seemed like you just passed out. You murmured a little, the way people who are drunk do sometimes." He ran a thumb over her cheek. "I talked them into just letting me take you home, said you were on medication that made you do that sometimes. But I really wonder if we should take you to the E.R."

She shook her head. "No. No doctors." Opening her eyes, she found his face close to hers, his breath warm and scented like an electrical storm. The spark of her arousal, which had never fully dimmed, flared higher. "I think...I think maybe being...turned on had something to do with it." She found herself putting an arm around him, pressing close and breathing deeply of the salty scent of leather and his skin. "I've never heard someone's thoughts before."

Looking up into his eyes, she hesitated a moment, but then tilted her mouth to his and kissed him. She forgot to close her eyes, watching him instead as her lips parted and her tongue coaxed his out to play. Desire flared hotter as he did, as he shifted them on the bed so that his arm went to the small of her back.

She was still in nothing but lingerie, he in nothing but leather pants, his coat shed somewhere in the house. "Touch me," she begged, breath quickening.

He slipped a hand into her panties again, gentle, so gentle, and as his finger touched her clit she heard his thought as clear as if he'd spoken it into her ear. *God, I shouldn't be doing this. What if she really does need a trip to the emergency room? She's a client, not a girlfriend. But how can I say no to her? How cruel would that be? To both of us. I know it's wrong, but it feels right. So very right.*

She concentrated herself on her breathing, on relaxing and opening up as each stroke of his hand spread her more. Then he whispered, "Do you want to come again?"

Yes, she thought. And the thought slipped out before she could even think to censor it, that Derek was the only person who'd ever made her come, not counting herself. There had been a little sex in college, and a very little since then, but none of it good, apparently. And she couldn't stop herself from thinking the earlier thought she'd had, about whether that gentle darting tongue would feel as good between her legs as it did between her lips.

He made a hungry sound and his weight shifted, he moved between her legs and she closed her eyes and pointed her toes as he slid her panties off. Warm breath crept into her pubic hair, then his fingers held her spread. She bent her knees more, canting her hips upward, and cried out softly at the first, moist lick, petal soft and slow-motion over her clit.

The more aroused she became, the tighter the connection seemed to be between their two minds. He sank into a trance-like state while licking her, though, no thought at all moving through his head in words, just feelings and impressions.

As she climbed higher and higher toward another climax, she let her mind imagine things. Imagine him with no clothes on at all. What his cock would feel like in her hand, what it would feel like pressing hard and hot against her hip, insistent and brimming with energy. She heard him moan and knew he saw what she saw.

She imagined his thumbs brushing softly over her nipples, and that there would be a twinge of pain when he entered her, but that his voice and his touch would soothe it all away.

"God, I want you." She wasn't sure which of them said the words, but it must have been her since she was the one whose mouth was unoccupied.

But he shook his head as he raised it, then went immediately back to what he was doing as he realized he didn't have to use his mouth to speak. *I want to, Wren. I really want to. But I'm not prepared. I don't have any condoms. And I'm not sure in the morning you'll—we'll—feel the same. Please, let's not rush.*

She gave a cry of frustration, jerking her hips urgently. She could feel his reluctance. She swallowed hard, and spoke aloud. "But I need you. God, please, Derek. You don't...I mean, maybe you shouldn't come, I know it's not safe, but...." *Oh, God, do you have any diseases I should know about?*

No, I don't, but even if I don't come, there's always a chance...

I can't explain it, I just know I need you. I need you to take me! She gripped him on either side of his jaw and pulled him up into a musky, slippery kiss, the flavor of her own juices mixing with the taste she was learning was him. *Please, Derek. It's...it's very important.*

She could feel him trying to resist, even as he was shucking the leather pants. *Important?*

She whimpered as his heated rod brushed her thigh. *I can't explain it. It's just intuition.*

He rubbed against her hip, groaning and breathing in her hair. *Then don't explain. Just imagine, or think, or KNOW. And I'll know, too.*

Wren felt herself slipping downward into deep water. "Hurry!"

He wanted to take it slowly, he wanted to breach her gradually, making sure she could accommodate him, making sure her pleasure was flowing. She could feel his plans, his desires, his fears, and feel them shatter at her word, her urge, as she wrapped her legs around him and gave him no choice but to plunge straight in.

"Wren!"

Her own scream got caught in her throat, the pain intense, almost blinding, and she knew he had felt it, too, as he trembled with the effort of holding still.

"Oh, God, Wren...."

It's all right, it's all right, it's all right. But it wasn't all right. It had hurt, *God*, it had hurt, and now they were both afraid to move.

But at least she was there, not in the dream world. She was present there in his bed, pinned in place by his cock. She saw light dawn in his eyes as the idea of it moved from her head to his. *In my dreams, there's a man. But....*

She couldn't explain it in words, but as Derek said, she could *know* it. Somehow she knew it was right that if Derek was the one she wanted, then Derek needed to be the one inside her. Claiming her. She drew a shuddering breath and tried to pull him deeper, but another agonizing spear lanced through her.

He shook his head and leaned very carefully to kiss her without moving his hips, then eased himself out of her. *I told you we shouldn't rush.* His eyes were wide with concern. *When was the last time you had sex?*

Couple of years ago. She couldn't even hold back the thought that she masturbated from time to time—and more often lately because of the dreams—but never used a dildo or anything. It was freeing, in a way, to not be able to hide anything, not to be able to hide the thought that she didn't even slip a finger inside herself when she touched herself. *It's okay. I think that was enough for now.* Meaning those few moments of penetration were enough to work whatever magic it was her subconscious wanted.

And what had her dream lover said? Entry was all that mattered, and it didn't matter which part of him or which part of her?

Derek made a sound and she realized he had just seen and heard a piece of her dreams. She shook herself. Her arousal was fading back to a simmer, and his thoughts sounded more distant as she heard him contemplate finishing himself off in the bathroom.

"No." She pushed him aside and pressed herself against him. "Teach me how to touch you." She found one of his hands with her own and interlaced their fingers briefly, before pulling it to his eager erection. She wrapped her fingers around it and thought, *God, no wonder.* He felt larger than she'd imagined. Then, her eyes locked on his, she began to stroke.

Chapter Five

SHE ARRIVED home early Monday morning, sore and restless, to find Lawrence weeding the front walk with a pair of office scissors and a worried expression on his face. Derek had barely backed out of the driveway when Lawrence had pulled her into a hug. Wren sighed. A nice dose of platonic energy grounded her. "Let's make some tea," Lawrence said. "Do you need breakfast? Are you rushing off to work? You have to tell me all about it."

Wren let herself be pulled into his condo. "Were you out there waiting for me to come in?" she asked, as she sat gratefully on his overstuffed couch while he fussed with the water and things. "It's only eight in the morning."

"Well, but the walk did need trimming," he said in a way that made it clear he meant *yes, I was waiting for you* but couldn't bring himself to say it outright.

She waited until he joined her, carrying a tray with cups and saucers and a large tea cozy shaped like a cat with one paw upraised, from which the tea poured. He took his own with sugar and milk and left her to treat her own cup as she liked. There were scones, she saw, but she wasn't hungry.

"Well, we went." She lifted the cup unadulterated to her nose and breathed deeply, the steam redolent of roses, sending a jolt through her. She took a careful sip. Yes, roses…and the images of her dream seemed very real. "What kind of tea is this?"

"Oh, it's some rose-scent black from Harrod's. My mother sent it last Christmas," Lawrence said.

"All right." She relaxed slightly; it wasn't a waking dream or her imagination. Now, this would be the real test, wouldn't it? If she could tell someone, and if they'd believe her. "I think I read his mind last night. And he read mine."

Lawrence grinned. "So, I take it more than just sleuthing took place?"

Wren blushed. "Oh, well, um, yes. But that's not what I was getting at. Oh, I'd better start at the beginning." She decided to add just a drop of milk, sipped a bit more, and then told him all about meeting Suzanne in the dressing room and all the gossip about sex clubs the older couple told them. Before she could get too shy, she explained the different rooms, how much deeper in there was a room for kinkier things, like using sex toys, and that there were specialty salons after that, one for women only, one for people who liked "messy" sex, whatever that was, and so on. Lawrence drank in every lascivious detail with such happy enthusiasm it was easy to go on.

She described getting turned on, and how she'd asked Derek to kiss her, "you know, so we'd fit in," and how it had been all downhill from there. The next thing she knew, he was making her come. "And while that was going on, I had thought he was whispering to me, but he wasn't. I was hearing his thoughts," she finished. "Like, we could have a conversation, back and forth, neither of us moving our mouths."

Lawrence was holding his teacup but he wasn't paying any attention to it. His gaze was fixed on her face, and when she looked up for his reaction, he just blinked. "That's...wow." He finally looked down into his tea. "So, he's amazingly hot, he's good in bed, he's the catch of the year, and he's a mind-reader?"

Wren almost spilled her tea. "What? No. At least, I don't think so. Lawrence, I'm the mind-reader."

"Oh!" Lawrence brightened at the idea. "But, had that ever happened to you before?"

She took a steadying sip. Goodness, but tea was a good idea. "No. Or, if it did, it was so mild I didn't notice the effect. None of my previous boyfriends made me feel that way."

Lawrence shrugged. "Maybe it's love? Oh God, I'm sorry, is it too early to use the L word?"

She let out a long breath. "It's lust, at the very least. And you might be right. It might have something to do with him, too, but I'm pretty sure it's me." She rubbed her temple with one hand. "But meanwhile, we didn't find my sister. I kind of...passed out when I came and he took me back to his place quickly after that."

Lawrence set his cup down and began picking apart a scone on a plate with his fingers. "Well, it is possible to come so hard you black out. For a man, anyway." He sounded a bit envious.

Wren's stomach grumbled and she took up a scone, too, nibbling on it. Maybe that was what happened? Hmm. Or the combination of the rum and everything. She would need to find out. "Anyway, I guess we have to go back, if we're going to find Abby, and I just don't know how this works, now that we've...been together." She blushed hard, thinking of how shamelessly she'd begged him to take her, only to have him exit after the first thrust because she couldn't bear it. "I mean, it's not exactly a secret anymore that we like each other."

Lawrence chuckled. "It wasn't a secret before, except that you had plausible deniability. But hell, now you've even read his mind." He set aside the plate of crumbs, all that was left of the scone which he'd managed to somehow inhale while Wren had talked. "But don't you have the perfect tool for what you want now? If your power works when you're turned on, and the sex club is where you need to search...?"

She sighed. "Yes, I suppose so."

"What's wrong?"

"Still weirded out by the thought of having sex with people watching," she said. Somehow having an orgasm in a room full of people who were fondling each other seemed okay, whereas what awaited them in the next room still seemed daunting. She added in a halting voice. "We...we didn't really... do it. Yet. Either." She finished her scone quickly. "And that's the last I'm telling you for a while! I better get to my meeting, or make the decision to call in sick."

Lawrence laughed. "You know that with me there's no such thing as Too Much Information." He stood, waving a hand vaguely over the tea things. "I've got this. You go on." But as he walked her to the door, he asked, "When are you seeing him next?"

"I don't know. We didn't say. I...I figure I'll rest out to-night. And maybe experiment."

"Experiment?"

"You know. I'll play with myself and see if I can peer into your wicked thoughts." She tweaked his ear playfully.

"Wren! All right. That was Too Much Information. If you want to order take-out or something, knock on my door."

She was chuckling as she went up to her own place, took a quick shower, and then went off to work. Talking with Lawrence made everything feel almost normal. That feeling lasted all the way until she reached her desk, where she saw the vase between her keyboard and monitor.

A blood-red rose with thorns still on the stem stood alone in the glass.

* * * *

She was distracted and nervous during the staff meeting. The meetings were fairly pointless for her anyway since she rarely interacted with any of the other library staff in her position. Wren had a feeling the meetings were an excuse to keep coffee and cookies in the department budget. Staying in the back of the room, she nodded without really listening to what they were discussing, then took two chocolate chip cookies in a napkin back to her desk afterward and contemplated what to do with the rose.

After staring at it for so long her fingers went numb where she was sitting on them, she got up and threw the stem into the trash barrel at the end of the hall, then put the vase into the supply closet behind the unopened packages of sticky notes.

Out of sight, out of mind. Right? If only it were true. She managed to bury herself for a few hours in manuscript conversion but kept wondering what the reaction of her secret admirer was going to be when he discovered the vase gone. It couldn't be Steve, could it? It had to be someone else. Unless Steve was like a Jekyll and Hyde type who was all mousy and timid in person, but in his dreams was like—well, was like the lover in her dreams.

She shook her head. It had to be a coincidence, the rose in her dream and the rose on her desk. Had to be.

Just like it was a coincidence that Uncle Herbert had a heart attack? Lawrence believed her when she told him she'd read Derek's mind. Why couldn't she believe herself?

Because believing that someone else was coming into her dreams and doing the things they did to her there was too frightening to contemplate, that's why.

She sighed. Steve himself was about the least threatening person she could imagine, but the unknown was always threatening. *Maybe I really should just meet him for coffee. Demystify the whole thing. I'll tell him I've got a boyfriend, but we can be friends.*

She went out to the lobby to make the call. His number was still in the call log, though she hadn't saved it under his name. She wondered if she should. Well, maybe if it seemed like a good idea after they met, then she would.

It rang. She wondered what department in the university he worked in.

When he answered he sounded startled to be getting a call. "H-Hello?"

"Steve, it's Wren."

"Oh wow, um, how are you?"

"I'm good. Look, I was thinking, do you still want to get together for coffee? I haven't had lunch yet."

"Oh!" He was flabbergasted for a few moments. "Um, yes! Except, actually, I can't get away right now. But I could totally meet you at like four-thirty or five?"

Four-thirty. She could keep from going nuts until then. "Sure. Four-thirty at the Starbucks across from the science center?"

"Yes. Yes, thank you. I mean, see you then."

God, he sounded like a nervous wreck. Wren hated the thought that she was going to ruin his day, but she just didn't want this hanging over her any more. She forced herself to concentrate on her work for another few hours, then gave up and surfed the Web for cute cartoons to e-mail to Derek. At four-fifteen, she slipped her jacket on and headed out the door.

A crisp autumn wind was blowing leaves off the trees and she looked around, wishing she had a hat but grateful her hair was too short to blow in her eyes. *I'll be lazy,* she thought, *and drive around to that side of the campus.*

She got in the car, the wind cutting off as she shut the door, her ears ringing slightly. It took almost as long to drive there as to walk, of course, because instead of walking straight across the campus, she had to drive around the edge, but ten minutes later she was circling the block looking for a place to park. There were people sitting in the window of the coffee shop, students working on their laptops and taking notes. A musician-type in leather jacket and long waves of auburn hair was just going in. She wondered which one was Steve, or if he was even there yet.

She went around the block once more, nervousness rising.

The jangle in her nerves suddenly lifted, though, as she realized with a certainty that she should not go in. She blinked, stopping the car at a stop sign, but just sitting there a moment. She couldn't see what would happen if she did go through with the meeting, but she knew she shouldn't.

Something wasn't right.

The car behind her honked and she jumped. No, she wasn't going in there. She'd go home. And call Derek. And then maybe Steve to apologize, but Derek first. In fact, halfway home she pulled over and called him.

"I'm worried," was all she said.

"Do you want to come here, or should I meet you somewhere?"

"I'll come there."

Finding his house was not that difficult, and in no time she found herself ringing his doorbell. He opened it quickly, as if he'd been waiting near the door. "Hey."

"I feel like I'm being stalked," she blurted out.

His smile was reassuring rather than condescending. "Probably best to talk about that inside instead of on the stoop," he said gently. "Have you eaten?"

"No, but I'm not hungry," she said as she followed him into the living room. Wren hadn't taken much notice of the room that morning. The furniture was bland but new-looking, as if it had been hardly used. He steered her to the couch and took her hand as they sat. "There was a rose," she began.

"In your dream?"

"Yes. And on my desk this morning."

His eyes narrowed. "And you don't think this is a coincidence. Couldn't you have just had a prophetic dream, though? How does that lead to you being stalked?"

"Let me tell you about Steve." She explained the halting phone calls, the fake one first, then the one asking her to coffee, then the feeling she had today when driving to meet him. "That alone would be weird enough, but then there are these flowers. Someone's been leaving them for me at my desk, and then they kept showing up in my dreams. I thought...I thought seeing them in my dreams was just my subconscious telling me to, you know, stop waiting around. But this time there was the rose first, in the dream I had at the club last night, and it looked a lot like it could be the same rose I found on my desk today. I suppose it could be my ability to see the future, that instead of seeing yesterday's flower, I see tomorrow's."

Derek let out a long breath.

"You think I'm crazy," she said, but it didn't look like he did. She just had to say that.

He shook his head. "You remember I told you I'm working on a missing person besides your sister? One of the things her husband found that made him think she was cheating on him before she disappeared was a collection of flowers. She told him they came from a secret admirer."

Wren squeezed his fingers. "Do you think she was kidnapped? Abby, too? And I'm next?"

He folded her hand inside both of his. "Slow down, slow down. Jumping to conclusions isn't always best unless your intuition is telling you something special."

She took a deep breath, trying to feel whether it was. "Hmm, no, I don't think so. It just seemed, well—what do you think the connection is?"

He thought a moment. "Well, the one connection is that I went to the club looking for the other missing woman, and

I thought I saw Abby there. Tenuous at best, and nothing at all if it turns out I was wrong. As for you and the other woman, there are the flowers, but we don't know if she was having dreams. Maybe you are somehow connecting with the dreams of the person who is sending the flowers in a way that's unique to your power?"

"Could be." She relaxed a little. Not only did Derek make a lot of sense, just being with him made her feel safe. And now she was sitting here close enough to smell his soap, with her hand going damp inside his. "I wish...I wish I knew more about it."

"About what?"

"My ability." She turned the pieces over in her mind, Abby, herself, the missing woman. "Doesn't it seem like kind of a big coincidence that you thought you saw my sister in the place you were already looking for your other missing person?"

"I admit, it does."

"But it makes sense if, well..." She hoped he wouldn't take this the wrong way. "What if my intuition led me to you in the first place? To the person who was already looking where the person I wanted found could be found. Then it's not a coincidence at all."

He was grinning. "That is, if that really was your sister I saw. But you've pretty much convinced me now that it had to be."

She smiled back. "So we were fated to meet, then."

"Must be." He looked so happy. He always seemed so open, so ready for anything.

She decided to make a suggestion. "We might need to, um, you know."

He raised an eyebrow. "I'm not the mind-reader."

"Experiment," she blurted. "Especially, I mean, so I don't, you know, pass out every time."

Now he smiled in spite of himself. "You know, it's okay to just ask. We don't – I don't need an excuse to be with you, Wren."

"Okay. But don't you agree? I...I really like you, Derek, and I really...want you." Just saying it sent a deep throb of desire through her. "But, we need to know. Especially if we're going to go back to that place."

"All right, you're right," he said, running the tips of his fingers around the curve of her ear. "Would now be a good time?"

She swallowed. "Now would be an excellent time."

He tilted her chin up to kiss her, just brushing his lips past hers at first, warming them. He spoke in a half-whisper, lips touching hers as he did. "First, we'll find out if it works without the rum."

He kissed her breathless, her desire mounting with each passing moment, but so far, his thoughts seemed inaccessible to her. "The bedroom," she whispered. "Can we go in there?"

"Of course." He held her hand as they climbed the stairs and went into the room. She took a deep breath. His scent was everywhere in the air here.

He sat her on the bed, slipping the cardigan sweater from her shoulders and then undoing the buttons of her shirt one by one, pausing to caress each newly exposed bit of flesh, until he urged her to lie back and let his hands slip over her already taut nipples. She was still wearing the shirt, and it somehow made her feel even more exposed to his touch than just being naked. She rubbed her knees together and made a hungry sound. "Want you."

He clucked his tongue. "I'm trying to be scientific here. One thing at a time."

"Ohhhh." Her answer was both plaintive and rapturous, as he caught one of her nipples between his lips and rasped his tongue over it. He repeated the treatment on the other side and she gasped. It almost felt as if she could come from just that, if he kept going.

But still no thoughts. "Maybe..." She had to catch her breath. "Maybe you have to be aroused, too."

He chuckled, lifting his head so she could see the amused look on his face. "Oh, trust me, I'm plenty aroused." He licked his lips. "Was that a fantasy of yours I saw last night, or was it just wishful thinking on my part, that you'd like it if I licked you?"

Her eyes were round. "I imagined it. And then you did it."

"Was it your first time being licked like that?" He undid her fly and slid her trousers down her legs, then returned to slip her panties off.

"Not my first time being licked," she answered breathily. "But first time being licked *like that*."

As she parted her thighs, he settled carefully between them. "For science," he said seriously, and then dipped his mouth toward her crotch, his eyes still looking up at her.

They closed as Wren felt the first velvet-soft sweep, and her eyes closed too. The next touch exposed her clit more, and she moaned as a gentle, moist touch made her legs tremble.

She forgot to listen for his thoughts as he lapped at her, his slow, teasing licks giving way to quicker movements. His fingers spread her more, and the tip of his tongue was wicked as it flickered over that nub, making her cry out.

Wren could feel how wet she was, too, and before she had quite realized it, she was thinking she wanted him to put a finger inside her, just to see, but she couldn't quite ask for that.

She didn't have to. He slipped an index finger in slowly, and it moved easily and without pain. She was sore, but the penetration was soothing as he moved it in and out of her. *Oh, God, that feels good.*

Do you want a second one? I'm thinking of just keeping it to one for now. No need to rush.

Her answer was to cry out again as she leaped up to another level of arousal. Maybe he was right, and they should take it slow. If nothing else, she should trust him. Trust him to take it slow when she wanted to rush.

And she cried out again, orgasm suddenly upon her as he sucked her clit between his teeth and flicked it hard with his tongue. *Oh, but wouldn't it feel good to...* She cried out again as he read that thought almost before it formed into words, biting her there, but gently, just a nip of teeth sending her into a second orgasm even stronger than the first, while his tongue did not let up.

A third orgasm hit as he crooked the finger inside her, tongue still lapping, but more softly now, and then he pulled his hand free and just lapped more and more slowly until every trace of tension or spasm was gone from her body.

He climbed up to the pillow and cradled her close. *Doesn't look like you passed out this time.*

Hmm, no, and so far, no dream or vision either. Although I am a bit sleepy now.

Sleep, then. I'll hold you. We can experiment more when you wake up.

All right. She slipped into a lovely, dreamless sleep.

* * * *

Derek's kitchen was larger than hers, but then, the whole house was. She drifted out of the kitchen and through the dining room and into the living room. The place was large enough for a family of four, but as far as Wren could tell, he lived there alone. On the mantel she found a photo of him and a woman on a mountainside, dressed for hiking. He looked younger in the picture, maybe college-aged? There was one that had to be his parents, standing together on the front steps of a house. She couldn't quite tell if it was *this* house, but it looked like it certainly could be.

She smiled. He was humming to himself while he cooked, accompanied by the sound of steak sizzling in a hot pan. She went back in to see if she could help with anything.

Soon she had the table set in the dining room, the two places set at one corner of the table, and rummaging through the sideboard, she had even found a lone candlestick with a taper and some matches. She lit the candle, then went back to the kitchen to find him covering the steak under a pot lid and throwing washed spinach into the pan the steak had just come out of. The water on the spinach popped like firecrackers as it met the hot fat in the pan and she stepped back. The microwave beeped.

"Do you like your potato with butter or sour cream?" he asked, turning the spinach with two wooden spoons. "I have both, I think. Well, check and make sure the sour cream is still good."

She checked, looking into his fridge with curiosity. A lot of jars of condiments, but it looked like he had some actual food, cheese and cold cuts, a few eggs, half a head of lettuce. Normal stuff. Not that she expected anything else, but she felt learning what was in someone's cupboards was part of getting to really know them. Pretty soon she'd find out how, or if, he folded his socks.

"Looks like butter," she said, when the sour cream container proved to be more colorful on the inside than it ought to have been. "I like butter better anyway. The sour cream is always too cold on the hot potato."

He had pulled the potatoes out of the microwave and set them on plates. He apportioned the spinach, now wilted down to what seemed like just two spoonfuls, and then cut the steak in half, putting one chunk on each. "There we go."

She carried the plates in, and he brought in a bottle of wine she hadn't noticed him opening. Too busy snooping around, she thought with a smile at herself. He poured a little into each glass. It was a rich, ruby red in the candlelight, and she lifted her glass and clinked it against his. "To dinner," she said.

"I'll drink to that." He took a sip.

Wren did, too. "I don't know anything about wine."

"Me either." He laughed. "A client gave me this bottle and said it would go good with steak, though. But I really haven't wanted to open it alone. The whole drinking alone being pathetic thing."

She wasn't sure what to say to that, only that it seemed impossible that this sweet, good-looking man wasn't already taken. "You live here all by yourself?"

"Yeah." He cut off a piece of steak and chewed it while glancing around as if looking at the place for the first time. "I had a roommate for a while, but he moved in with a girlfriend about two months ago. I should really move to a smaller place, but..." He shrugged. "The place is all paid off, and the taxes aren't that bad."

"And moving is a pain in the butt," Wren said, cutting open her potato and slathering butter in. "It's nice, though. A pretty big house, quiet street, but you're still so close to downtown."

"I know. Not that I really use the office all that much. It's mostly just a place to meet clients since I don't want most of them to know where I live. My real office is downstairs, my files and everything. But it's nice to be close, easy to get to." He looked up suddenly. "Which reminds me."

"What?" She paused, a forkful of spinach stuck in mid-air.

"I don't know if you've been wondering how it works professionally versus personally. I mean, now that we're..." A flush crept up his cheeks that had nothing to do with the wine. She could see him struggling to describe their relationship without rushing things ahead merely by invoking words like "girlfriend" or even "relationship."

"Now that we've kind of shifted from professional to personal," he finally said.

"Yeah, I did kind of wonder." She set her fork back down. "Though it's far from at the front of my mind. Or it was, until you brought it up."

He smiled, laughing softly at himself. "Well, anyway, it doesn't have to be a complicated ethical issue. Just don't pay me."

"Oh." She thought about that. Was it really that simple? "Are you sure?"

"If things had happened the other way around, if we'd met some other way, there's nothing I've done to search for Abby that I wouldn't have gladly done for anyone I cared about, right? And I'd certainly never charge family or friends for helping them." He took a deep breath as if he might need to steel himself for her reaction.

"Okay." She found herself smiling. She didn't want to pin words on it either, this new fragile thing that was blossoming between them. But he cared about her. That was nice to hear. Even if she already knew it, knew it beyond any doubt since, after all, she'd been in his mind. "So you don't have to stop trying to find Abby, and we don't have to stop doing what we're doing."

"No."

"Good." She started to eat again, a thrill twisting through her gut as she wondered when they'd finally do it. She nearly opened her mouth to say something, then decided to let the fire simmer in her belly a bit longer. They still had practice to do, after all, didn't they? And there were still several days before the next night they could visit the club, plenty of time to work on it. She had some ideas, some definite ideas, but she could tell Derek about them in bed.

She ran one foot up his leg, though, as they were coming close to finishing eating, something she'd never done to anyone before. He groaned as if hungry, and she knew it wasn't for steak. What would it be like for him to just grab her now and take her, there on the table, both of their desires stoked so high it would be like two thunderclouds meeting and exploding in a strike of undeniable power?

Her foot, clad only in a cotton sock, worked its way to his crotch and she massaged the hardening length of him. The ridge of his erection filled the whole arch of her foot, her toes curling around the head.

She felt suddenly ashamed. "You didn't come yet." She had drifted off to sleep in his arms after he'd brought her to orgasm after orgasm this afternoon, and only realized now that he must be aching to come himself.

"It's all right..." he said, with some difficulty, as her foot had not stopped moving. He gripped the arms of his chair, though. "I figure my patience will be rewarded."

She slipped out of her own chair and urged him to move his back from the table as she knelt between his knees. She tugged at the button on his jeans for a while before he finally reached up, his hands covering hers for a moment as he undid it for her.

The zipper she handled herself, revealing the shape of his cock molded in cotton by his briefs, one shiny spot there where fluid from the tip had soaked through the fabric. She leaned down to suck on that spot and found it enticingly salty. Soon, a much larger area of cloth was soaked as she licked and sucked the whole head of his cock through his underwear, until his groans took on an edge of desperation. She eased the elastic waistband up and over to reveal the dark red flesh.

She lapped at him with long, slow licks, drawing longer groans out of him. Long, slow licks like the ones he'd used on her. She wondered, would he respond the way she did if she got faster, and flicked her tongue back and forth more quickly, and maybe used just a little bit of teeth to...?

The sudden bitter spurt made her cry out in surprise. The second squirt streaked her forehead and went into her hair. As she rocked back on her heels, she let go of the edge of his waistband and the rest of his load ended up in his shorts. "Oh, God, I'm sorry!" She put a hand over her mouth. "I didn't mean...."

"To give me the most amazing blowjob I've ever had? Sure you did." He pulled her up into a kiss, and she could taste the mingled flavors on her tongue, smell that crackled ozone scent of his breath. "God, Wren, the things you do to me."

"How long...how long..." But her throat tightened up and she couldn't finish the question. She felt his arms tighten around her.

"When you're ready," he whispered. "I'll be inside you when you're ready."

She nodded, breathless, wanting the time to be *now* but knowing it wasn't.

"Let's get in the shower," he whispered back. "I think we both need one now."

Chapter Six

_____

THEY WERE in his bed, the feather comforter pulled up around them and Wren nestled against his chest, when she remembered the dream. "I wonder...I wonder if I'll have another one," she said, too warm and secure at the moment to feel any real apprehension over it. "Or if being with you will keep the dreams at bay."

He stroked her hair. "Nothing seemed to stop that one at the club," he said softly, sounding almost reluctant to bring it up.

"True." She rubbed her cheek against his chest. "But that was before you...before we..." She couldn't come up with the right words for it.

Derek did. "Before I was inside you?"

"Yes."

"You think it really will make a difference?"

"It feels like it, anyway." She hugged him hard around the ribs. "I want...I want to do it before we go back to the club. We should, right? Go back on Sunday to look around more?"

He pressed a kiss against her hair. "Seems like it. And you'd be helping me with my other case by coming with me, too."

"And I should practice." She watched a patch of light move across the ceiling as a car went by outside. Such a quiet neighborhood. "I want to figure out if I can really read other people when we're... you know. Or if it's only you."

"It seems like...."

"I know what it seems like. But we ought to test it." Wren nuzzled against him, trying to work up the nerve to tell him her idea.

"How?"

"I think you should come to my house tomorrow night. And we should test it on Lawrence." There, she'd said it, but she was blushing.

Derek was silent, and her desire was sated and quiet; she could not hear what he was thinking at all.

"He knows. I already told him," Wren went on. "About the mind-reading. I figure, just a little test, like he could be reading a book, and I'll see if I can tell what book. We'll tell him when it's going to happen so he can, um, not think about anything he might not want me to know. Right?"

Derek chuckled. "That might guarantee he thinks about it. But, you're right. If he'll go along with it, it's the best way to test it. It does mean telling him we're having sex, though."

"I know." Wren raised her head to look at him. "Normally that'd flip me out. But compared to the thought that this is working up to you...us...at the club, well...."

He pulled her back down, fingers kneading the back of her neck. "Point taken. Tomorrow night, then, your house, if Lawrence agrees, you'll test your abilities, and we'll...."

Wren raised her head again. "We'll what?"

"We'll get one step closer to what you want. My cock. In you." His eyes were dark in the amber glow from the street lights. "Can you say it, Wren?"

She reached down to find the bulge in his pajama bottoms. It was soft, but the bulk of it was still impressive in her palm. "Your cock," she whispered, a thrill worming through her core. "In me." She leaned toward him and pressed her mouth to his. "By Friday."

He let out a breathy laugh. "I'll put it in my Day Planner." She nestled back down in the crook of his arm and he asked, "So you'll stay tonight?"

She nodded. "I'll go by my place in the morning for clothes before work. Other than the Monday morning meeting, they couldn't care less about what time I get there."

He hummed happily, the sound reverberating in his chest and in Wren's ear where she was pressed against him.

* * * *

She dreamed. She dreamed she was the princess of a fairy kingdom, and Derek was the prince from a neighboring kingdom. The king was upset that Derek had tried to have sex with her, and he was captured and brought into the court. He was strapped down, tied naked to a table in front of the king's throne, all the courtiers looking on. Wren sat on a small throne of her own, but she could not move, could not speak, as the king ordered his mage to step forth and test the prince. The mage was Lawrence, and he waved a magic wand that made Derek's cock stand up tall, and then it began to glow. Just the first two inches glowed a bright blue, and the brighter it glowed, the harder Wren's own clit throbbed. Lawrence was explaining, in a very high-class British accent, that these two inches were the two inches that had made it inside the princess.

The king seemed to ponder this, then decreed that the offending two inches should be removed, and the prince's life spared. The king called for his sword. and while waiting for a knight to bring it, with much trepidation, Wren was trying to get Lawrence's attention to free her from the spell that held her in the throne when she woke up.

She woke to find her hand on Derek's cock, massaging it. He was fully hard, but seemed to be asleep. It was still dark, and she couldn't see over him to the clock. She kept her hand where it was, stroking him as she shifted onto her stomach and slipped her other hand under her and into her panties.

She was sopping wet already, and a few thrusts of her hips had her slick fingers raking over her clit on each push. She could not hold back a moan, and Derek answered with a groan of his own.

He pressed against her then, and she had to let go as his cock rubbed insistently against her hip. Before she realized what was happening, he had shifted on top of her, his cock rubbing against her tailbone, pre-come slicking the skin.

She thrust up against him, moving her hips to her own rhythm, so close to coming already. His own soon matched her, his weight and heat pressing her deliciously into the bed.

What was in his mind? What was he dreaming? She felt herself opening up to let his thoughts in. Did he have elaborate dreams of kings and castles?

But what she found in his mind was just the thought of rutting, dreaming of exactly this. He was not awake.

That didn't make it any less hot for Wren. She imagined that instead of pressing against her, he was inside her, the tip of his cock parting her folds, the bulk of him molding her insides to fit him, each thrust going deeper and deeper....

She came silently, biting the pillow, shuddering under him, wondering if he came in his dream if he would come in real life, or if there was no difference, since his dreaming mind was wholly taken with the sensory input? Her fingers worked again, pinching her clit between them, a second orgasm cresting over her first, and she imagined it, the explosive spasm of him inside her, coming inside her...

She pushed into his dream and then cried out in surprise when instantly the cock against her back began to spurt. That woke him, a sudden flicker of awareness.

Wren!

It's all right. We're just dreaming. Well, we've both come, but it's a dream.

God, some dream....

I know. I liked it, though.

Mm. Me, too.

And then sleep dragged them both down again. Wren smiled. She could be a dream-lover, too, it seemed. Her dreams later that night were of Derek and only Derek.

* * * *

She arrived at work slightly later than usual the next morning. For a half-second she looked around for the vase before she remembered she'd put it in the supply closet. There was no flower, no note from Steve, nothing to say he was upset about her standing him up. She wondered if she should have called with some excuse for why she hadn't shown up, but by now it was too late for that. Maybe she should at least apologize.

Why not tell him the truth? Or part of it, anyway? *I really wanted to meet you, but when I got there, I just couldn't bring myself to go in.* He was shy, too. He'd assume that was why.

He didn't call. She didn't feel stalked when she went out to grab lunch. By mid-afternoon, she had forgotten him, thinking instead about Derek and wondering what exactly they were going to do tonight.

She knocked on Lawrence's door with a pizza at a little before six o'clock.

"Oh my God, is that sausage I smell?" he said. "You're a lifesaver. I skipped lunch and I'm starving."

They settled at Lawrence's dining table. His place had the same layout as Wren's, but he had divided his living room into the sitting area around the TV and the dining area with a nice table, matching chairs, and a sideboard. That was where Wren had her desk, a bookshelf, and the treadmill.

"Can I ask you a favor?" she asked when they were each well into their second slice. "You can say no."

He rolled his eyes. "Whenever you say I can say no, I always feel like then I can't."

"Well, that's hardly my fault," she teased. "It's about tonight."

"Tonight?"

"Derek's coming over and I want to do a bit of an experiment." She slapped him on the back of the hand when he leered. "That's not the kind of experimentation I mean. Derek's straight."

"Are you sure? He could be bi. Have you asked?"

"*No*, I haven't asked!"

"Then are you sure? He dresses pretty nicely for a straight guy."

"Lawrence!"

"Okay, okay, what's the favor?" He bit into his pizza with a Cheshire-Cat grin.

She took a breath, hoping to explain it calmly and with a minimum of embarrassment. "I want to try reading your mind."

"Right now?"

"No. No, later. Since I have to be, you know, for it to work." She was blushing but not so badly that she wanted to hide her face. She pressed on before he could say anything more. "But I don't want to pry if it does work, so I thought, you could be reading a book."

"I did just buy that new David Baldacci...."

"No! Don't tell me what it is!" She made an exasperated sound. "The whole point is to see if I can tell what book you're reading."

"Ahh. Okay." Lawrence took a swig of Coke straight from the can. "And if I'm reading a book, presumably I won't be thinking about my own deep, dark secrets?"

"Yes." She wiped her hands on a napkin. "Does that mean you'll do it?"

"Sure. How will I know when to start reading and when to stop?"

"Well, he's supposed to be here at eight," Wren said, checking her watch. It was barely six-fifteen and she was tempted to call Derek and tell him to just come as quickly as he could.

Lawrence appraised her. "So you'll be doing the nasty by, what, eight-fifteen?"

Wren blushed deeply this time. "Um, probably."

"The 'why-do-we-ever-leave-the-bed-at-all' stage is one of the best parts about a new boyfriend," he said sagely. "It's all right, Wren. I'll start reading when I hear him go up the stairs. I'll read until around nine unless I hear differently from you."

* * * *

Wren excused herself soon after that, not wanting to smell like sausage pizza when Derek arrived. She took a quick shower, then dug out a few things from the cabinet underneath the sink.

There they were, a box of tealights, each little white candle in its little aluminum cup. Digging a little deeper, she found the thing Abby had given her for Christmas three years ago, a little clay pot and stand, and a bottle of scented oil. A tealight went into the base and would heat the oil and scent the air. The oil was supposed to be gardenia-scented. She wasn't sure if it really smelled like any actual flower, but it was pleasant.

She set it on a plate on her dresser, arranging a half-dozen of the tealights around it and lighting them. Very pleased with the effect, she turned off the overhead light and put on the reading light by the bed.

That reminded her of something else. She pulled open the side drawer and rummaged around. Yes. She pulled out a small cardboard box and looked in it. Yes, two condoms. It was a three-pack a previous date had left here after having used only one of them. They were two years old, but according to the dates on the foil, they should still be okay to use.

She left the two square packages conspicuously on the side table. Just in case.

With the room prepared, that left Wren wondering what she should wear. It seemed silly to get dressed just to get undressed again, but at the same time she couldn't quite imagine being so brazen as to lie in bed naked, waiting for him.

She blinked as she realized that was exactly what she had just imagined. The sheets would be cool against her bare skin as she slid between them. She felt a surge of desire throb low in her abdomen.

But he wasn't going to be here for another half-hour, and she'd have to get up and answer the door when he arrived anyway. She pulled on a bathrobe as a compromise, the terrycloth rubbing against her nipples and ass. She sat down with a book of her own to wait.

It wasn't long, it seemed, before she heard his SUV pulling into the parking space behind the condo, and before she knew it she had run all the way down three flights of stairs to meet him at the door.

He pulled her into a hug, there on the threshold, and she felt the chilly autumn air creep up the open bottom of the robe. A moment later, his hand moved in a circle over her bottom, as if polishing it with the soft terry, his eyes searching hers wordlessly. Questioning but approving of her lack of attire.

Upstairs he had just set down his overnight bag, and she had only just shut the door and latched it, when she felt his hands on her waist from behind, undoing the belt of the robe. "The bedroom," she said, but fell silent as he kissed the back of her bare neck, then suckled hungrily at the spot under her ear that always made her melt. His hands parted the robe and let it fall to the floor between their feet, his fingers skimming her already hard nipples.

"I talked to Lawrence," she said, breathless but determined.

"Good." It came out little more than a growl. "Wren."

"The bedroom," she said again, whispering it this time.

"Yes." He picked her up and carried her.

The gentle scent of the oil was heady now that it had been heating for a while, exotic and intoxicating, but no more so than the taste of him, the scent of his breath, as he lay her down on the bed and kissed her, finally.

She lost track of time during the kiss, lost track of their hands, losing herself completely in it. When he spoke, he was hoarse, as if he hadn't spoken for hours, though it couldn't have been *that* long. "You like my tongue," he said—not a question, but a statement.

"Very much."

"Let's start there," he breathed, kissing her one last time, and then leaving a trail of kisses down her torso.

As with the time before, he began slowly, lapping with long, soft strokes until the hard bud of her clit was revealed, then narrowing his attention to it with quicker flicks of his tongue tip. But just as her arousal was reaching a peak, he spread her lips with both hands and stretched his tongue into her.

She gasped. So that was what he meant by starting there. She had never felt anything like it, so muscular but flexible, pressing into her and awakening nerve endings all around her opening. It felt so good. She tried to spread her legs wider, to let him go deeper, and his chin pressed hard against her as he tried to get as much of his tongue going in and out of her as possible.

I can't believe I never thought of this before.

His surprise was evident. *You haven't?*

It just didn't occur to me that you could...fuck with your tongue. Or that anyone would fuck ME with their tongue. Just regular head seemed like too much to hope for most of the time.

She could feel his disbelief, and as the belief sank in, a kind of disappointment in his fellow man, and then he brought his attention back to her clit.

Oh God, she was close.

Of course you are. I can feel it. He chuckled and backed off, lifting his head and wiping his chin before planting a soft kiss on her mons. *So what's Lawrence reading?*

"Um..." She closed her eyes, feeling for Lawrence, for something.

Yes. There he was. Wren burst out laughing and Derek joined her. "Is that what I think it is?" he asked.

"I told him not to read the David Baldacci book he's in the middle of," Wren said. "Because I already knew that. But I had no idea he liked Harry Potter."

"Everyone likes Harry Potter," Derek said seriously. *Now, let's see about getting you off.*

No, wait! You're not even undressed yet.

Is there something wrong with that?

Well, no. But yes. I want to feel your skin, Derek. I want to be making love, not just experimenting. We don't have to be "doing it" to both be part of it, do we?

She imagined them in a sixty-nine and felt his cock jump in her mind.

All right. It's a good idea, but I want to add something to it. I want you to come with something in you, and my finger will be awkward at that angle.

He got off the bed, shedding his clothes as he made his way to his overnight bag. She giggled as he attempted to hide the thing he took out of it, as if to surprise her, but she could see it perfectly well in his thoughts.

Chagrined, he brought it to the bed, kicking off his socks as he went. He placed it in her hand. It was a small, soft, rubbery thing, shaped like a dolphin leaping out of the water, the "water" being the flared base of it. The material felt silky, almost warm instead of cold the way plastic would feel, and was lavender in the candlelight. It wasn't even half the size of him, but it was larger than one of his fingers.

Come here, he urged her gently, lying back on the bed and guiding her into position. She was on all fours above him, brushing his erection with her lips. She felt him sit up partway and press his mouth to her opening again, tongue snaking out as if to ensure the way was still slick.

Here you are, came his thought as he spread her lips carefully with one hand and then slid the toy inside her.

Ohhhhh....

She squeezed it, feeling it with her muscles, as it warmed up to her temperature. And then his tongue found her clit again and she cried out softly.

She tried to concentrate on his cock for a while, lapping it and sucking it, but this position wasn't as good for that as she'd imagined it would be. Their heights didn't quite match up. She kept trying, but she didn't think she'd make him come this way, while he was pushing her inexorably toward orgasm. As she grew close, she heard his thought, *leave it*, and she lifted her mouth free to cry out while he brought her off, his tongue working like a demon's until she spasmed. Then one hand drew the dolphin halfway out and pressed it back in slowly, over and over.

I want you, I want you, why can't I have you yet?

He hushed her. "No rushing. It would kill me to hurt you, Wren. Don't push, okay?"

"Okay..." She felt as if some thought in his head moved out from under her, like some leviathan in the deep water she couldn't see into. "Your turn to come, though."

"Oh, no argument there," he said.

"Then hush, and lie still." She crawled off him and settled between his legs. Yes. He fit much better into her mouth this direction. She lapped up a salty gem of pre-come and slid the whole head of his cock into her mouth.

"God..." *Her inexperience is completely made up for by the fact that she can read my arousal.*

I heard that!

He groaned as she knew exactly where to press her fingers behind his balls, exactly how fast to move her mouth and how hard to suck to bring him off, and wasted no time in doing so.

* * * *

The next morning she woke to find the little dolphin standing on the side table next to the two condoms, and a note from Derek.

Sorry I had to rush off.

Had to meet a client.
I'll be back tonight.
Don't forget to ask Lawrence what he was reading.
-D

Wren yawned. She'd slept through his phone ringing, then? She had only a vague sense that she had been dreaming. She didn't remember anything.

The day at work passed in a blur. There were no phone calls from Steve, no mysterious flower deliveries, and a very badly scanned manuscript to deal with, so she was actually surprised to find it past five when she looked up to see what time it was.

She assumed she'd see Derek at eight again, and she still had half a pizza left. She called Lawrence from her car on the way home and he insisted she come over again, and he'd make a salad so they weren't eating *just* pizza.

Lawrence's idea of a salad included goat cheese and walnuts and dried cranberries in addition to the vegetables. Wren found herself only eating one slice of pizza after the immense bowl he put in front of her. "So," she finally asked, when he was starting on his second piece, "was it Harry Potter?"

He laughed. "I thought you'd be amused." Then he blushed.

"Oh, God," Wren had a sudden thought. "When I could see what was in your head, could you see what was in mine?"

Lawrence looked up in surprise, "What? Oh, no. I had no idea when you did it. But I could hear you through the ceiling. And since I was supposed to be reading, I couldn't very well come in here and put on the news or something to drown it out, could I?"

Her own cheeks were bright, but she was uncowed. "At least we didn't keep you up."

"Not much, anyway," he admitted.

Wren tried to keep her thoughts on the experiment. "I wonder why Derek can hear me, then, but you couldn't?"

He wiped his lips with a napkin. "Well, were you trying to communicate something to me?"

"Hm, no."

"Perhaps that's why." He sat back with a sly look. "You could try that tonight. He's coming over, isn't he?"

Wren's blush deepened as another one of those rushes of desire went through her. "Yes. Yes, he is."

* * * *

She had arranged the room like before and was wearing only the bathrobe when her doorbell rang at quarter to eight. She went rushing down the stairs, wondering why she hadn't heard his car, but didn't realize until she'd pulled the door open that it wasn't him at all.

A slightly-balding man in a golf jacket and slacks was standing there with a clipboard. "Er, hi." He looked at the clipboard as if making sure of what he was saying. "Are you the resident of unit number three?"

"I am." He didn't have any logos on him like the pest control guy or like the environmental canvassers. But he seemed a little familiar. Maybe a neighbor? "Can I help you?"

"And your name is...Delacourt?" He looked as if he was trying to read the name on the buzzer and was making a bit of a production out of it.

"Yes," she said shortly. "Is there some kind of problem?" She held the top of the robe closed. "I'm kind of busy."

"Er, well..." He seemed at a loss, staring a bit oddly into her eyes, his own too wide as if willing her to go along with him. And he seemed nervous. Maybe he was just flustered by what she was wearing, or not wearing? "Um, I'm, um, from the local committee to increase voter participation. Are you registered to vote?"

"Yes, I'm registered already," she said.

"Oh. Good. Well, don't forget Election Day is coming up in a few weeks and, um, exercise your right to be part of the democratic process!" He took a step back. "Thanks for your time."

He made haste down the steps and Wren watched him walk toward the next house, catching sight of Derek's SUV as it came down the street.

He greeted her with a kiss and a close hug and she gasped. She could feel how hard he was right through the cloth of his trousers.

"I've been thinking about you," he whispered in her ear.

"Come upstairs," she said, pulling him by the hand.

She didn't let go until they were in the bedroom, and she pulled him down for a proper kiss. "We've got a new experiment to try," she said, when she caught her breath. "I'm going to try to send a thought to Lawrence this time instead of just receiving."

Derek pressed her backward until she was lying flat on the bed, then opened the robe and ran his hands up her body. "Any particular message?"

She worked at his belt with her hands as he crawled over her, kissing here and there. "Hmm, I hadn't thought of that.

But I probably should think of something, so what he gets isn't just, 'Oh my God, Derek is so hot!'"

He chuckled. "Is there something you've always meant to tell him but never could?"

"Oh, like does he know he's got dandruff or something? Sadly, Lawrence is perfect in every way and the only reason I've never asked him to marry me is he's gay." She waved a hand vaguely. "I suppose I could tell him I'm sorry the plant he gave me for Christmas two years ago actually died. You know that spider plant in the kitchen window? That's like the fourth one. I keep buying new ones and putting them in the same pot."

Derek laughed again. "Perfect."

"Me, or the idea?"

"Both."

"You're wearing too much."

Apparently he agreed, climbing off the bed to get undressed while she tossed the bathrobe to the floor and got under the covers. He fluffed a pillow and then slid in next to her. He put his arms around her, and she nuzzled against his chest, so warm and soft. She petted the sparse silky hairs there in the hollow of his breastbone. "So I've got my experiment for tonight," she said. "What's yours?"

"Hmm?" He made an innocent noise.

She clucked her tongue. "I can tell you're up to something, I just don't know what yet, because I'm not hot enough yet to read you."

He hummed hungrily. "Then maybe I ought to do something about it, and you can find out for yourself." He brushed his fingers past her already-stiff nipples, down to her mons. He cupped the furred bump and began rocking his hand slowly back and forth, just a half inch, no more. A circle with a tiny circumference.

She moaned. The touch was firm, but only tangential to her hottest spots, her clit hidden between her still-closed lips. But the gentle tug on the flesh was stimulating, and wetness gradually accumulated, slicking her parts so that each small circle caused a slight friction now, her lips parting and rubbing, and then without her quite realizing it was about to happen, his middle finger slipped into the wet slit, rubbing right over her twitching clit.

Wren moaned louder, and his fingers kept moving until that middle finger was buried to the second knuckle in her, and still his hand kept moving. She bucked against him then, and he slid deeper still as she ground her clit into the palm of his hand.

Right, the dead houseplant. She reached out for Lawrence, found him watching re-runs of *CSI*, and thought, *So I've been trying to hide the fact that the plant you gave me died. Now you know.*

But in the next instant she focused on Derek again. He'd hidden something under the pillow? What?

She pursued the thought until she caught it, then slipped a hand under the pillow to grasp something rubbery. Another dolphin?

He did not stop the movement of his hand as she pulled the toy out. This one was more penis-shaped, but still far from realistic, the same lavender as the other one, but just a gently undulating shape with a somewhat bulbous head when compared with the sleek nose of the dolphin.

The lady in the shop assured me this is the average size of the American male penis. Derek slid his finger all the way in.

But you're larger than this.

Exactly the point.

Wren understood his plan now. To stretch her out gradually until she could take him without pain. She felt her frustration mount. *You don't have to do this,* she thought. *It isn't that big a deal. I'm not made of glass. And it's not as if you're a Great Dane and I'm a Chihuahua.*

Please, Wren?

When he asked like that, though, just a plain, unadorned plea, she couldn't really say no, could she? And it wasn't as if she questioned how much he wanted her. She could feel that herself. She closed her eyes and again there was something there, large and dark in his mind, like something behind a curtain.

In fact, I'd like you to put it in.

Her eyes flew open. "You want me to what?"

He withdrew his hand and coated his own cock with the juices on his fingers, then scooted back a few inches, stroking himself.

Imagine it's me.

Wren pushed the covers down and reached between her legs with the dildo, rubbing it against herself until it was slick, and then aiming the blunt head at the place she knew it should go. She pushed, but her flesh resisted. It felt too blunt. *The dolphin first,* she thought.

He acquiesced, taking up the dolphin from the side table and slipping it into her inch by inch, fucking her with it carefully so that each time it sank in a bit further until it was all the way in. Then he pulled it back a few times, until it was almost all the way out of her, before pushing it slowly back in.

Yes, yes, like that.... that's just how you're going to do it with your cock, she thought. At her next thought, he pulled the smaller toy away and she replaced it with the bigger one. She imagined it was Derek's cock in her hand, that she was guiding the spongy head into place. It still took a push to get it to go, but then suddenly, the first two inches of it were buried in her. She cried out more in surprise than in pain, and then made another noise of surprise.

Derek was coming, silently but copiously, his mouth round but his eyes never closing as they roamed from the toy protruding from her body to her face.

* * * *

Much later, as they were drifting to sleep, Wren suddenly realized why the voter registration guy seemed to familiar. "Oh my God."

"Hm?" He pulled her close in the crook of his body, nuzzling at the back of her neck.

"I think that was my stalker."

"Who was?"

"Right before you showed up, a guy came to the door, acting really nervous. I wasn't really paying much attention to what he was saying, because I was thinking about you. I thought he was flustered because all I was wearing was a bathrobe." She could still picture him perfectly in her mind, slightly balding, his eyes wide. "I thought he seemed familiar, but I couldn't figure out from where. But it was Steve, the guy who has been calling me on the phone." Wren gripped Derek more tightly. "And that wasn't the house next door he was walking to when you drove up. It was the red minivan."

Derek was at the window peering out before she could stop him. "I don't see any van now."

She joined him, looking through the blinds. "It's gone. I've been wondering whose car that was and why they were never parked in a driveway." She couldn't quite remember, though—was it there on the nights she had dreams, and not there on the nights she didn't?

Derek pulled her close. "What was your impression of him?"

"Steve? Same as on the phone, actually," she said, resting her head against his chest. "Seems really, really sweet, but totally, totally vulnerable."

He pressed a kiss against her hair. "Just like you."

Wren gave a soft laugh. "He doesn't feel like a stalker, is what I mean."

"You'll call me if that van appears again? Don't approach it. Get the plate number if you can, but don't go near it."

His voice had a seriousness about it that made her shiver. "Okay. But he really did seem harmless."

"Wren." She listened to him breathe for a few breaths. "Your intuition about this dream lover drove you to...to hurt yourself. I don't know what the connection is between Steve and the dreams—maybe there isn't one. But I trust your intuition, which also told you not to meet with him. Be careful."

She pulled him toward the bed. "I will."

Chapter Seven

WREN WOKE to the sound of the shower running. Derek was obviously up already. She bit her lip, thinking about the night before, and slipped into the bathroom, breathing deeply the steam. Now that it was getting cold at night, the electric baseboard heaters in the condo made the air so very dry.

The tub was enclosed by a sliding door with crinkled patterns in the glass. She could see the flesh-colored outline of him as he rinsed his hair under the showerhead.

She stepped carefully into the back of the tub, sliding the door behind her and putting her hands around his waist, his skin deliciously hot and wet against hers. His arms went around her, cupping her still-dry buttocks, but as he pulled her into a kiss, water cascaded down her back.

They kissed long enough that Wren felt herself warming and liquefying inside, and she could not miss the opposite reaction from him, his cock hardening against her hip. When the kiss broke, he spoke. "Are you sore today?"

She took his hand and guided it to her mons, spreading her feet slightly. He extended his fingers, finding the pool of gathering cream there, circling the tip of his finger just inside her entrance. "Yes, a little," she said. "But it's a good sore. Makes me want more."

"Tonight," he promised. "There'll be more."

"And tomorrow?" she breathed.

"My Day Planner says tomorrow I've promised you all of me."

She pressed against his leg, then, her desire awakened and wanting to come now. He pressed his lips to her forehead, acquiescing without words to the question she asked with her body. He turned her so that his cock pressed against her tailbone, and his hands slid down her body until he could touch her clit. He had to bow his back, keeping one hand on her breastbone, holding her up while the other spread her lips and his middle finger sawed slowly back and forth.

Yes....

He brought her off quickly, only pausing every once in a while to dip his finger inside her and make her moan with desire. When she came, he held her against him, keeping her from sagging into the tub. He groaned quietly too, waiting for her aftershocks to subside, before he turned her again, guiding her hand to his swollen prick.

As she stroked him, he groaned again. *Something about us being connected...you made me come last night.*

Wasn't that the goal? she asked.

No, you triggered my orgasm from inside my head.

She knew that was what he had meant, but she had to tease anyway. *Want me to see if I can do it again now?*

He met her eyes, a light of challenge flickering in both their gazes. *Sure.*

She took her hands off his cock, and went up on her tiptoes, hugging him around the ribcage as she trapped his cock between her thighs. She could feel the hard length of him against the tender flesh of lips. *Kiss me.*

He obliged, his cock sliding a bit as he shifted lower to meet her mouth. She parted her lips, feeling a kind of energy crackle inside her, and then as his tongue darted into her mouth, she released it.

Oh God. His arms tightened around her and she felt the spasms and twitches of his prick. *Oh God, Wren.*

She held him until his breathing began to slow again. *Is it good that way?* She had to ask.

Yes, God, yes. But she could sense the unarticulated thought, that he believed it would be even better inside her, and she caught sight in his mind of the final toy he had bought to breach her with, which he planned to use tonight.

* * * *

She was getting dressed a short while later, and considering whether they ought to eat dinner together, when Derek looked up from his phone. "I just got some interesting e-mail," he said.

"What sort of interesting?"

"It's from Rhonda, the new member liaison at the club, inviting us to a special Halloween party at the place tomorrow." He looked up from where he sat on the edge of the bed, his features neutral.

Wren raised an eyebrow. "Halloween party?"

"It says they normally wouldn't let us attend on a night other than Sunday until after we'd been there three times, but Suzanne and Bob vouched for us, and they really want a full house for the event, I guess." He raised an eyebrow back at her.

Wren thought a moment. Friday night they had plans, but maybe she could convince him they ought to do that tonight. She felt her chances of convincing him were going to be better in the heat of the moment, though, than if she said something now, so she kept the thought to herself. "Why not? If everyone's there, that'll be our best chance to see if Abby or this other woman you've been looking for are there, right?"

"Well, that's true." Now he looked at her thoughtfully, and she wondered if he were thinking about their plan for Friday night also. "But it's really your decision."

She hesitated only a moment. "I might even have a costume."

"Oh, I hadn't thought of that."

She slid open the closet door and rummaged in the back. "Yes! How about this?" She pulled out a very, very short flapper dress, covered in fringe. A matching headband was looped over the top of the hanger. Who else but Abby had convinced her to get it, so they could go together to a party once a very long time ago? Wren couldn't even remember now if it had been a Halloween party or just a 1920s-themed thing.

Derek came and put an arm around her waist. "It's perfect. I hope you have a long coat, though. It's supposed to be cold all weekend."

"What about you? What are you going to wear?"

He slipped his phone into his pocket. "I suppose I have a cowboy hat in the closet. And I think I have a vest. With the leather pants that should be okay."

She grinned, trying to imagine him in a cowboy hat. "Sure." For a moment she didn't think about the more serious reasons they were looking into the club, or even the sex, but just that it would be fun. She went on tiptoe to kiss him. "See you tonight. Come earlier? Come at six and bring dinner."

He smiled. "All right."

Wren went with him to the door, to give him one more goodbye kiss, and opened it to find a small green box sitting on the landing.

Derek snatched it up, then laughed, handing it to her. "It's a box of fertilizer for houseplants."

"Miracle-Gro? I guess this means Lawrence heard the message."

"Seems that way. See you at six."

She didn't want to stop kissing him, didn't want to see him leave. Calling in sick seemed like a better and better idea. What was it Lawrence had called it—the "why-do-we-ever-leave-the-bed-at-all" stage? But then Derek was headed down the stairs, and there was no point in staying in bed *alone* so she went to get ready for work.

* * * *

That night, Derek arrived slightly late, six-fifteen or so, citing traffic as the reason, but Wren suspected it was because he'd bought enough food for a small army. His arms were laden with take-out from an Italian place near downtown that had a dinner counter, and he'd brought a small pan of lasagna along with salad, Italian wedding soup, garlic bread, a fried ravioli appetizer, and tiramisu in cups for dessert. And a bottle of Chianti wrapped in rope.

Knowing they were going to eat first, Wren had kept her clothes on, and they chatted their way through the meal much as they had before they'd begun having sex, only this time she felt the tension shifting and building instead of just simmering underneath. He plucked a tiny meatball out of his soup and offered it to her. She took it in her mouth with delicate care, her tongue slipping between his fingertips.

Upon eating the last of the ravioli, she declared herself too full for dessert. Derek assured her it would make a fine snack later, and packed it away into the fridge. Between them they had barely eaten half of what he had brought, and Wren wondered how many lunches she could get out of it.

That was her last thought that wasn't about sex for a while, because the moment everything was put away and the counter wiped, she led the way to the bedroom. While he visited the bathroom, she lit the candles and refilled the little pot of scented oil, and was just considering whether to take her clothes off herself, or wait for him, when he emerged.

"Let me," he said, when she reached for the buttons on her shirt. He sat on the bed and pulled her to stand between his knees, while he undid one button at a time, nuzzling in the hollow between her breasts as he worked his way down. He undid the cuffs at her wrists, kissing the pulse point of each before slipping the shirt from her shoulders.

Now he ran his finger just under the satin edge of her bra, undoing the clasp in front as he looked up at her, his hands slipping to cover the flesh he exposed. She shivered, but not with cold.

His mouth went to one nipple while his hands worked the button of her fly, and her pants slid easily down her legs. Her panties he pulled down just to her knees. His palms drew wide, warm circles on her asscheeks, and he bent his head to breathe warmly into her dark thatch. "Wren...."

She reached out for him in her head, but the connection was not yet clear. She could sense him, but not hear his thoughts, as if he were still too far away. His hands roamed up and down her skin, and she could feel his desire flickering like a torch all over her.

The heat rose in her everywhere he looked, everywhere he touched, as if she were some exotic work of art he was appraising without even fully unwrapping. Somehow her panties hanging from her knees made her feel more exposed than if she'd merely been nude. "Why am I always the one undressed first?" she whispered jokingly.

His head jerked up, a hint of alarm in his eyes before he blinked it away. "I thought you liked it."

"I do," she said, wondering why she was blushing now. It felt dirty and good at the same time, somehow, to be naked while he was still fully clothed. "It makes me feel..." How to describe it? Like a naughty little girl? Like a slut? Like a sex object? She wanted him to just *know* those thoughts, which made more sense as thoughts than as words, but the connection was still fuzzy, she could tell.

He pulled her close, pressing his cheek against her bosom. She could feel a tinge of sadness, of regret. That something he had hidden deep in his mind.

"It's sexy," she whispered reassuringly. "It makes me feel wanted."

She imagined unzipping his fly and taking his cock out right there, and just climbing onto him, joining their bodies without him even taking off anything, his arms around her, holding her against him. The throbbing between her legs was her own pulse, but she remembered the feeling of his cock pressed there, stiff and straining.

He tilted his head back, looking up into her eyes. "I want you."

"That's convenient," she said, feeling as if she was saying a line from a movie, though she couldn't think of which one, "because I want you too."

She pushed him back onto the bed playfully, hoping to lighten his sudden somber mood, and began to wrestle him out of his clothes. He gave in with a laugh, helping her to get them off with a minimum of damage to them. She wrapped her hand around the bulk of his cock, stroking it up and down. It really felt as if it had a bone in it, and there was something enticingly exciting about that.

"What did you bring this time?" She had seen just a glimpse of it in his mind that morning, but now she doubted the image she held, which had seemed to be of a cock made of ice.

"I'll show you." He slipped off the bed and retrieved a long velvet pouch from his overnight bag. He placed it in her hands as he settled beside her again. Hmm. The bag felt as if it had a bone in it, a very dense, heavy bone.

She slipped it out of the case and found a beautiful piece of glass sculpture in her hand. That it was the approximate shape of a penis hardly mattered. It had a glittering swirl through its center, like she expected to find in glass unicorns sold in Disneyland. "It's gorgeous."

"And utterly smooth, dense, and rigid," he said, sounding as if he might have been quoting a salesperson. "Even if it's not quite as large as me."

She stroked him again and then held them side by side to compare. Down toward the base, the glass phallus was almost as wide around as Derek was, a gradual and graceful taper.

She handed it back to him and lay on her back, a silent request.

He leaned over to kiss her, one hand slipping between her legs to slicken her folds and clit with her own wetness. They both groaned into the kiss as he slid a finger into her and her hips bucked upward. *Put it in me.*

I think you should do it.

I think YOU should do it. You won't hurt me, Derek. You won't.

He hissed softly and she felt his fear.

You won't hurt me, she repeated. *You'll feel what I feel. You'll know.*

I know I'll feel what you feel, Wren. When I hurt you....

His thoughts tangled into an unreadable mass of confusion. Wren took the hand of his that held the toy and bent her leg, guiding him until the tip of it rested just at her opening. Looking into his eyes, she pulled on his wrist, the slick hardness of the glass entering her inch by inch. She drew a deep breath. The glass was deliciously cool, and so smooth there was no friction at all, just a feeling of being steadily filled. Penetrated. As it slid deeper, her lips parted and she panted, as the feeling of being stretched by it began to grow.

Then it was seated all the way in, and while she held it in place, two of his fingers bumped over her clit. *It feels huge,* she thought, meaning her clit, not the thing inside her, as if by displacing her flesh it had somehow pushed more blood, more everything, into the once-tiny nub. She shuddered as he dragged his fingers over the swollen flesh again, and one of her hands caught hold of his cock.

They touched and stroked each other for a while that way, but Wren's hand was not half so busy as her mind as she slipped deeper into his thoughts, unraveling the knot of fear and confusion bit by bit as his arousal mounted and his attention was drawn away.

She pulled the glass partway free and pushed it in again, moaning at the smooth slide into her. But what she wanted was Derek, hot and hard and joined with her. *Surely I'm stretched enough now?* She'd never been so stretched in her life, but it felt nothing but good.

Deeper. She pushed the glass deeper, and even as she did so, she delved deeper into Derek's mind.

Finally, she felt she had somehow reached a threshold. She whispered, "What are you so afraid of?"

It was as if someone turned on a light in a dark room full of pictures she previously had not been able to see. He made a distressed sound, as he realized that these things he'd been avoiding thinking about were exactly what he was now thinking about, and that Wren could see it all.

Katy had been her name. Wren was absorbed in the flash of a memory, his hands holding her firm by the hips, her legs wrapped around him as his cock sank into sweetness, but her scream making his skin go cold, adrenaline flooding him....

It had been like that every time. Three times only did they try to have intercourse, contenting each other with oral sex and petting without ever speaking aloud about what they were avoiding. The first time had been the night he'd proposed to her. They'd both been virgins. She'd blamed it on being too soon after her period. She always had trouble around then, she said. The second time had been two weeks later, and they'd gotten drunk first, but if anything the pain was even worse, given her reaction.

The third time she was on top, and she could hardly bring herself to go past that first inch, trembling and crying, and Derek babbling back at her about how they didn't have to, she didn't have to, but she forced herself down....

She left during the night, leaving the ring behind. He didn't hear from her for a year, and then it was a Christmas card with a Canadian address, saying she was about to move to England.

Wren found herself pulling him close, her hands cradling his face and kissing him. The salt of his tears was in her mouth, and that only made her kiss him harder.

That won't happen. I'm not her. It's not your fault. But she could feel her thoughts bouncing off the memories as if they were encased in glass. The past couldn't be argued with and it couldn't be changed. Neither could the fact that Derek blamed himself. Never mind that Wren was pretty sure he wasn't so huge as to be regularly injurious to a partner. Never mind that it seemed the woman had never gone to a doctor about it, even though she had said her period caused her pain. They had been too young, too afraid of each other, too afraid to talk to anyone about it.

No wonder he was so afraid of hurting her.

She pushed him onto his back, the glass sliding out of her as she reared up on her knees and climbed atop him.

No, Wren, no! A jumble of thoughts came hard on the heels of his fear: *not yet not yet at least use a condom just because you're ready doesn't mean I am...*

"Shhhhhhh." She made a shushing sound, to emphasize it. She stroked her hands down his face, over his chest, then nuzzled him on all fours. One hand reached under her to stroke him again, gone half soft in the face of his traumatic memories. He hardened under her touch, though, his mind quieting.

She settled herself over him, her hands on his chest, the head of his cock peeking out from under her bush. She rocked forward and back, dragging her clit up and down the length of him. He was anything but glass, hot and rough and pulsing. She rubbed against him that way, faster and faster, rolling her hips, until they were both nearly at the brink, and then she backed off, slowing, lifting herself up with her thighs, brushing instead of pressing with steady friction, luxuriating in the sensation.

Want you in me. I don't think I can be any more ready.

A sudden chirping filled the room and he groaned. The moment he did, Wren knew why. That was Diana's ring tone, the one that meant urgent. Wren was so deep in his mind she caught the full idea then, that he'd hired Diana to do some of the work on the Helena Riggs case, because he'd been spending so much time with Wren.

She hadn't known the name of the missing woman before now.

If only you could read Diana's thoughts from here and tell me if it's a false alarm. He was flooded half with regret, half with relief as he slipped out from under her and dug the phone out of the pocket of his pants.

Wren lay back on the bed, the glass dildo poking her in the back. She let it distract her from his thoughts, pulling back into her own head as she examined the beautiful pattern in it again. She could still hear what he was saying, though.

"The hospital? He's what?"

Wren could hear the distress in his voice.

"You're kidding me. Please tell me you're...no, no, it's all right. I...Yeah. I'll get down there right away. I have...a hunch this might be hard to prove, though."

He sat back down on the edge of the bed.

"Helena Riggs?" Wren asked. "I'm sorry, I didn't mean to pry, but...."

He chuckled softly and pulled her close for a kiss. "Her husband is the councilman I told you about. That was Diana. She's at the hospital. He's had some kind of seizure and he's lost consciousness. She didn't use the word coma, but they're saying right now it doesn't look like a stroke, and they can't determine the cause." He looked at her for a long moment.

Staring into his eyes like that, even with the peak of desire ebbing away, Wren couldn't help but read his thoughts. He was thinking that if she had the power to make him come, what other effects could a telepath have on someone else's nervous system? Maybe without even being in the same room? He was already convinced there was a connection between Abby's disappearance and the Riggs case, and that someone was stalking Wren through her *dreams*, and now Jim Riggs was in a coma? Had he been stalked, too?

She backed across the bed until they were no longer touching. He was afraid. Not of her exactly, but afraid nonetheless, of so many things, and fear was always a cloud.

For some reason, it made her angry. "Can't have you going off to the hospital like that," she said, licking her lips. But instead of reaching for his erection with her hand, she just pushed at it with her mind.

He threw his head back and let out a pained groan as he spurted, untouched, white streaks painting the clenching muscles of his belly.

When the orgasm ended, he was panting, and he rested his hands on his thighs for a few moments while he gathered himself. "I don't...I don't know if I'll be back tonight."

"I know." She wanted to say she'd go with him, grab her coat, whatever. But she wasn't even supposed to know as much as she did. "I'll be okay." *But will you?*

The connection was too faded for the thought to go anywhere but the inside of her own skull. "I'm sorry," she whispered, as he stood and went toward the bathroom. *I didn't mean to scare you.*

But she had. She'd forced him to show her things he hadn't wanted to, and then she'd even made him come without touching him, just when he was starting to wonder if abilities like hers could be used to harm.

He dressed quickly and then leaned over the bed to press a tentative kiss against her forehead. "I'll call you in the morning."

Meaning he wouldn't be back tonight no matter what happened at the hospital. "It's okay," she said, even though she wasn't sure it would be. What else could she say? "Be careful."

"I will."

And then he was gone, and Wren fell back against the pillow, all desire she'd had to come herself completely evaporated.

* * * *

She opened her eyes and found herself in the cone of white light. *Oh, shit.* It was nearly blinding, and this time she squinted to try to see beyond it. In the darkness beyond, colors swam, but she could not tell if she saw faces there, or only the colors in her own eyelids.

She looked down—she was naked, of course. There between her legs on the floor was a bouquet of gardenias, their scent mingling with the scent of her own desire. Her hands were behind her back, and she turned her head to look behind her.

Someone clucked his tongue, his hand grasping her by the chin and forcing her to look straight ahead again. Cloth whispered against her hair as he tied the blindfold and she could feel the warmth of his body against hers, and the rough sensation of his clothes.

"Who is he, Wren?" came the voice, right in her ear, a melodious purr. "If he really wanted you, he wouldn't have left you like this, would he?"

She tried not to think about Derek, about what she'd seen, about why he'd left, why he wouldn't be back. Not tonight, anyway.

There was a low chuckle in her ear. "He's not the one for you. You need someone who *fits* you." Again, a chuckle at his own joke.

His hands slid down the valleys of her thighs, one spreading her wide, the other reaching a finger down to saw at her clit. She gasped at how sensitive she was.

But as her arousal mounted, she reached out with her mind, trying to answer for herself once and for all if her dream lover was real, or just a strange expression of her subconscious desires and fears.

Again the chuckle, as a finger slipped inside her. "You need it, your body needs it. You feel it, the biological imperative. You're wired to want to be fucked. There's nothing wrong with that."

Wren bit her lip. She couldn't feel another person, couldn't feel another set of thoughts, not like she did with Derek.

"Beg me to fuck you and you'll come like you've never come before."

No. No, whatever her mind was trying to tell her, if it was trying to express her need, her frustration. She had to talk to Derek. She had to find out what he was thinking and see if he would be willing to try again. Maybe if she promised him she wouldn't fish around in his memories....

"No," she said aloud in the dream.

But the fingers were still touching her, still pushing her arousal. "Do you really mean that, Wren? What if he doesn't come back? Why turn me away? I only want to make you feel good. To give you what you need."

She woke suddenly to find her own fingers were rubbing her clit sore. She gritted her teeth and came with a cry as her alarm clock went off.

Chapter Eight

THERE WERE no gardenias on her desk when she arrived at work, which left her questioning even more whether there was anything to her dreams other than her subconscious fears and desires trying to find voice. Some of them were suppressed with good reason, she decided.

Shortly after lunch she gave up working and left early. Walking across the campus, she passed students dressed as robots, vampires, and angels, plus one whole group of sorority sisters who appeared to be a swarm of bees. Halloween wasn't until the following Wednesday, but the students were celebrating while the weekend was here.

There had been no call from Derek. She wasn't sure whether to feel relieved or annoyed, and instead felt both. She sat in the car staring at her phone for a while, relieved the inevitable difficult conversation wasn't at hand yet, and annoyed that he hadn't called like he'd said he would.

Could he still be at the hospital? She dialed his number, deciding that at the very least, she should try to talk to him instead of just stewing. It went straight to voice mail and Wren hung up.

She wasn't sure why she decided to call his office number next. Just a whim? She was shocked when someone answered, a woman's voice.

"Private investigators, may I help you?"

"Um, hi," Wren said hesitantly. "I'm a client of Derek Chapman's?"

"He's not in at the moment."

Wren had a sudden thought. "Is this Diana?"

"It is. Is this Ms. Delacourt?"

"It is." Wren blinked. "He told you my name?"

"Under strict confidentiality, I assure you, ma'am," Diana said. "He was up all night at the hospital. I finally forced him to go home and get some sleep. I turned his phone off when he wasn't looking. I planned to go wake him up around six."

"Oh. You don't have to do that. I could do it. He and I are supposed to go somewhere tonight." Wren wondered how much Diana knew about their plans.

"Do you have a key to his place?"

"No, I don't."

"Come by the office and I'll give you one."

Wren soon found herself face to face with Diana, who had some sort of paperwork spread all over the office's main desk and a large pot of coffee sitting on the percolator. She had shoulder-length brown hair, and despite wearing a baggy sweatshirt and jeans, she exuded a decidedly feminine aura of authority. She had dark circles under her eyes as she smiled to greet Wren. Then she went into a side office Wren hadn't even noticed the first time she'd been there and rummaged in the desk, then came back out with a keychain shaped like a dinosaur.

But instead of just handing it to her, Diana sat in the same chair Derek had sat in and looked up at Wren tiredly until Wren sat, too.

"Derek really, really, really likes you," Diana began. "Neither of us slept much last night, and most of what we did while not sleeping was talk. That is to say, he talked about you while I listened."

"Oh."

Diana gave Wren a motherly smile, though she didn't look old enough to actually be Wren's mother. "I've known Derek for several years now. He's a good guy, but he's had rotten luck with women. Or maybe just rotten women."

"I know he proposed to a girl in college," Wren said. "But it didn't work out. She left him, but he blames himself."

Diana nodded. "That sounds like him. He was celibate for a long time, that much I know. And he had a girlfriend for a while when we first met, who was sort of a golddigger, except she wasn't really in it for the money, but for the drama. She didn't really care about him per se. She kind of got off on him talking about his dead parents and wanting to 'be there' for him when he needed her. I think she was disappointed he didn't wake up sobbing in the middle of the night every night. And as far as I can tell, they almost never had sex. She was a withholder, for sure."

"A withholder?"

"You know. Always withholding it from him as a way to control him. Like a carrot on a stick, except she never rewarded him with the carrot. And he's just not the type to beg, you know? Then there was nobody for a long time, and the next one was the total opposite. She couldn't have cared less about how he felt about her. She just—well, this is going to sound crude, but I heard nearly the same thing come out of both of their mouths at different points. She was only interested in him because he had a big dick. And because he never said no. Never said he was too tired or didn't feel like it. So she was another one who just bossed him around, but in the opposite way as the previous one."

Diana shook her head. "And there was a string of women he met through blind dates, personal ads, Internet dating sites, none of which lasted beyond a single night. He gave that up, too."

Wren shrank down in her chair. *God, does he think I'm a nympho, insatiable? Am I too pushy? No one's ever accused me of being pushy before....*

"Now there's you," Diana said, her voice kind rather than accusing. "He's over the moon about you, you know."

"He's...I like him really a lot, too," Wren said. "I have a similar string of first dates. I'm just—I'm worried about him."

Diana put the keychain dinosaur into Wren's hand and closed her fingers over it. "Worried how?"

"I think...I think he's a little afraid of me."

Diana chuckled. "Of course he is. He's afraid he'll wake up one morning and you'll turn out to be just as bad as the others. But that's nothing to do with you. Aren't you afraid of the same thing?"

Wren looked up at her. "I...I guess I am. I think... think maybe we're both afraid of screwing it up."

Diana stood. "I don't know if it helps to say this, but try not to let that become a self-fulfilling prophecy, all right?

Don't be so afraid that you rob yourself of the chance to do it right. I know, I know—easy for me to say, not so easy to do. But I said it to him last night, and I'm saying it to you now."

Wren stood and smiled, imagining Diana admonishing Derek not to be afraid. "I'll go get changed for the party and then go wake him up," she said. "And thanks. I'll... we'll try to make things work out."

When she got back in the car, though, her optimism sagged. Diana didn't know the other reasons why Derek might be wary of her, did she? Probably not. She couldn't imagine Derek telling her his girlfriend could force him to come without touching him.

Wren had to talk to him, but at the same time it was getting close to party time, and she dreaded trying to either rush through the conversation or going to the party without figuring out some things about how they felt about each other.

She sat with her head leaning against the steering wheel until her forehead began to hurt. *Wait a second. If the main reason we're going to the club is to look for Abby....*

Why couldn't she go and ask around for herself? She wouldn't even have to lie. *I'm looking for my flaky sister who got burned out of her apartment a couple of months ago and I heard a rumor she might be working here.* If Abby was there, and she found her, she could certainly find out from her whether Mrs. Riggs might have been there, too.

Yes, that made perfect sense. Didn't it?

She tried to call Derek again, but again it went straight to voice mail. Right. Didn't Diana say she turned his phone off?

Wren imagined waking him up with the news that she'd found her sister and Helena Riggs. All the trouble would be over and then she could make up with him with a clear head.

She started the engine and headed for the club.

* * * *

The parking lot was empty when she pulled in, but she continued around behind the building and found four cars parked in the back. That seemed like a good sign. Surely some workers were there early to set up? She parked and was about to put her phone into her purse when she realized they might be suspicious of the camera on her phone. She put her purse and phone into the glove compartment and shut it, then got out of the car, stuffing her keys in her jacket pocket.

There was an unmarked door at the top of a small set of stairs, next to a loading bay that was closed. She pulled on the handle and the door opened.

"Hello?" she called.

No answer. She went a little deeper in, wondering how far she would have to go before she reached one of the rooms she had been in before. She was in a service hallway, the paint drab and cracked, a fluorescent tube flickering overhead. Various doors lined the hall on one side.

She knocked on the first one she came to. "Hello? Hello?"

The door was pulled in abruptly and she found herself face to face with a man, bare-chested and barefoot, wearing just black track pants. His skin was the color of creamy coffee and his hair was hidden under a black bandanna. He looked her up and down. "Can I help you?"

"Um, no. I'm looking for somebody who works here." Wren smiled and tried to look harmless.

He shifted from foot to foot. "Yeah, well, um, the guys don't really get here for another hour or so."

Guys? "No no, my sister. Abby. Although she might be using a nickname or something."

"Abby isn't already a nickname?" His look of suspicion deepened.

"Er, well, yes, but..." She took a deep breath and tried to stay focused. "Are there some other people I could talk to? It's really important that I find her." But it came out sounding like a lie to Wren. Apparently it sounded that way to him too, because he cocked his head and looked at her askance.

Then he seemed to make some kind of decision. "Come on."

He led her through what was clearly a dressing room into a small lounge area. The couches were draped with sheets, but it looked more like a backstage area than one of the public rooms Wren had seen before. "Wait here," he said, then closed the door behind him.

Wren sat on the edge of one of the couches, looking around the small room. There were two dressing room mirrors attached to the wall opposite her, one horizontal at about the height of her head and one upright. For checking makeup and costumes? There was another door facing the one she'd come through, and she guessed it must lead out to the public areas.

She sighed, hoping the guy was going to get some other employees for her to talk to. This would be so much easier, she thought, if she just could have been reading his mind from the start. Maybe she should have masturbated in the car before coming in. She wasn't certain that would have worked, but it seemed now as if it ought to have.

She clenched her thighs. Just how aroused did she have to be for it to work? She slipped off her jacket and laid it aside, brushing her hands over her blouse. Oh, that might be too visible, but then, did she care if some guy stared at her tits if she got the answers she was looking for?

She rubbed her hand over her mons through her skirt, a frustratingly unsatisfying touch, but the frustration only seemed to arouse her faster.

The man who'd greeted her burst in. "I knew it." He grabbed her by the arm. "All right, come on. Let's get this over with."

Wren reached out, but her sight hadn't sharpened yet. She couldn't sense his thoughts really, but he was exuding a feeling of giving in to what she wanted. His grip was tight on her arm as he marched her through the other door and into a room set with what looked like the tables in the gynecologist's office. He threw a sheet over one of them and pulled her into a sitting position atop it.

It was only when he strapped her wrists in place with wide, heavy leather straps that she began to think there was some misunderstanding. "What are you doing?"

"Just be patient," he said, an exasperated edge to his voice. "It's a pain when people show up early. And I don't know you, so I can't be too careful."

"But, but I...." While she tried to make sense of what he was saying, trying to reconcile it with the emotions she read from him—resignation, annoyance, disdain, a tinge of disgust—he pushed her back and strapped her ankles into the stirrups. One of his fingers slipped under the edge of her now-exposed panties and he ran the back of his fingernail up and down under the edge of the cloth.

"Wow. You're dripping for it already." He shook his head in disbelief. "I'd do you myself, but I don't have the knack that Evan does, and you'd just be back in a couple of hours begging for more."

"Who's Evan? What are you talking about?"

"Don't act like a nut job," he said as he secured a blind-fold around her eyes. She could feel a wave of dismissal in his feelings, but also a strangely sweet thread of kindness. "You'll get banned and then where would you be? I've seen what happens and it isn't pretty." She could feel him con-sidering, then felt something hard and rubber being pressed between her lips. "Come on, here you go. Now you won't say anything crazy."

He thought he was doing her a favor, protecting her. That feeling came through clearly and she was so surprised by it, she opened her mouth and let him put the gag in place.

The door closed. Obviously he thought she had come here seeking sex of some kind. The truth was the opposite. She'd come here to avoid having to have sex here later, but there was no arguing that point now.

She would have to let Evan, whoever that was, arouse her more, and then she could speak directly to his mind about what was going on. Meanwhile she counted the seconds, then the minutes, while she waited.

At last she heard the door open.

"And did you get her name?" A man's voice, almost fa-miliar, like a voice she heard in commercials or something.

"No, I didn't. I didn't recognize her, Evan, but it seemed obvious enough to me what she wanted."

"Thank you, Ramon. You may leave me to it."

The door closed again, and Wren flinched as she felt a hand on her shoulder.

"Shh, shh," he said, close to her ear. "No need to be afraid. Everything will feel much much better very soon." His hand brushed down over her blouse, circling one nipple until it stood hard against the fabric. "You must forgive Ramon. He thinks all you need is a cock inside you." He clucked his tongue. "Didn't even bother to undress you. He fails to understand that you crave something more than just a full cunt. Which is exactly why you come to me."

Wren felt the buttons being opened on her blouse, then the open air on her breasts. His mouth was shockingly hot after the cool air, and his tongue rasped over one nipple, then the other. She moaned around the gag.

"Yes, it's good, isn't it?" Then she felt something hard against the inner side of her thigh, cold like metal, and then there was a tugging on her underwear, and a tearing sound. Had he just cut away her panties with a knife?

His fingers massaged the wet flesh there, spreading her lips and dipping just barely into the opening. She tried reaching out again, focusing her thoughts and trying to hear his. She would have to convince him he wasn't hallucinating, wasn't just hearing voices....

Can you hear me? Stop, please stop, it's all a mistake.

She heard his voice answer, as clear as a bell in her mind, even as she heard the sound of his belt buckle being undone. *Now, now, none of that. You'll feel better and everything will be much clearer in a little while.*

Wren was stunned. She knew that voice. She hadn't quite recognized it with her ears, but in her head she felt the shock go through her whole body. Her dream lover. This was him in the flesh. *It's you!*

Of course it is. The head of his cock nosed at her opening, as he coated the head with her juices. Then she heard the sound of something tearing—a condom wrapper? Yes, as the head returned, feeling cold this time.

No, no, no! You must believe me. I didn't come here for sex. I'm just trying to find my missing sister.

She read the flicker of disbelief clearly, and the knowledge behind it. Sometimes women convinced themselves they were coming to Evan for some other reason. Sometimes quite ludicrous reasons. They could not admit they had become addicted to sex with him, and their minds invented delusions. He haunted their dreams, and after sleeping with him some women could find no pleasure in any other lover. It didn't happen to every woman, but maybe one out of ten or twenty....

But I've never had sex with you before! His fingers brushed over her clit as he teased her with the head even more, then slid it up and down over her clit hood. He began to thrust rhythmically, rubbing the head of his cock against her clit. She could feel her own orgasm building, even though she didn't much want to come. Well, she did. Her body did. But her mind was still in rebellion, even as she could feel his intention to take her to the very edge of orgasm before he would plunge his cock into her and open his mind to her in one coordinated moment.

She tried again. *You said you wouldn't until I was ready, until I begged you to!*

That got a reaction, the mental equivalent of a double-take. Finally, his question. *Who are you?*

It's Wren! Wren Delacourt. You've been visiting me in my dreams....

Quite abruptly, she found the blindfold lifted and she was staring up at a man with long auburn hair. It fell in curly waves partway down his chest. He reached up and unbuckled the gag, and let it fall, but he continued to speak to her with his mind. *So you're Wren.*

He was thinking that he hadn't known dreams could actually draw her there. His hand ran down her breastbone until his thumb could slip to the side and circle her nipple again. *You're trembling with need, Wren. And so am I.*

Please don't. That isn't why I came here. I'm just looking for my sister, Abby.

Ah, Abby, yes. He pulled back from her then, physically and mentally, so quickly it left her breathless and feeling a chill. She hadn't known it was possible to cut someone off mentally before. "If you'll excuse me," he said aloud, then wrapped his hand around his cock. "We have much to discuss, but I have a pressing need of my own. I'll go find your sister now, in fact."

He was still stroking himself when he left the room. And Wren was still strapped down, unable to move.

Chapter Nine

IN THE silence she stretched out her senses, listening and *listening*. But her heart wouldn't settle, and her thoughts beat against the insides of her skull like a moth in a jar. She tried to take a deep breath, but it was hard to relax with her legs spread and her own juices dripping.

Evan had to be a telepath, too, that much was obvious. And Abby was *here*? His final words had made it sound as if he was going to get off with Abby's assistance. So why had he been trying to seduce Wren in her dreams? Had Abby told him about her? If Evan had been wanting to meet her, why hadn't Abby just called and asked her to come over and meet him?

Because, Wren thought, *this situation was highly fucked up*. And Derek was asleep at home with his phone turned off. And her own was in her glove compartment.

She tried to imagine him lying asleep in his bed, his hair over his eyes. She tried to imagine lying there next to him, dripping wet, stroking him to hardness, and then whispering to him, *Derek. It's time. I need you.*

In her vision, his eyes opened and fixed on her, wide and slightly shocked.

"Okay, up you go." It was Ramon, and he removed her blindfold. "Need you to see where you're going."

He undid her wrist straps and moved her into a sitting position, then bound her wrists together behind her back. She looked into his thoughts; he had no suspicion of anything wrong, anyway. It was fairly normal for him to tie people up and not to think much of it. He didn't question the orders he had been given, and he was good with ropes. The thought that Wren might not have been a fully willing participant never even entered his mind. "Come on," he said, and helped her to her feet. "Leave your shoes. Let's go."

Well, Wren thought, *at least if I go along with this, I'll find out what the hell has been going on.*

He marched her in front of him through the room, into another room and down a dimly lit hallway. There they met Evan, now wearing a leather jacket, with a bit of a grin on his face. He led the way down a set of stairs and Wren nearly stumbled, the sense of deja vu was so strong.

That first dream? No, not a dream, the vision she'd had when she'd tried to use her sight to see Abby. The man with red hair and a leather jacket in front of her, her hands bound behind her.

She knew what was coming next. When they reached the bottom of the stairs, she was pushed to her knees, but she bowed her head and kept her teeth clenched tight. Looking straight down, she could see the grimy blue shag carpet and not much else.

Someone gasped. Wren looked up and there was Abby, one hand over her mouth, looking very wan and frail.

Her hair had grown long and it was tangled, and she was wearing a corset like Wren had seen the women who worked at the club wearing, just the tiniest bit of skirt ruffle around the edges, making it obvious she wasn't wearing any underwear. Regret poured off Abby in waves. Wren didn't dare open her mouth to say anything, though.

"Oh, Wren, I'm sorry. It wasn't supposed to happen like this."

Evan stepped between them. "Family reunion later, eh?"

Abby sank to the floor and was silent. Wren dared a glance at the other people in the room. She blinked in shock as she recognized the man standing off to one side, not from a dream, but from her front stoop. The voter registration canvasser. "Steve?" she said, too startled to remember to keep her mouth closed.

"Er, yeah, sorry about that," he stammered. "But, well, you didn't come to the coffee shop. But we had to meet somehow. And just seeing each other should have been enough."

Evan put a hand on Steve's shoulder. "Indeed, it should have been, but there are things beyond our understanding. Even if you didn't feel the legendary pull, the meld should still work."

Steve turned crimson. "Oh, I felt it. It just seems she didn't."

Evan patted him soothingly. "Get undressed. It'll be easier. Ramon, help her out of that skirt."

Wren stood and Ramon wrestled her out of her skirt and the rags of her underwear. Her blouse was now around her wrists with the bindings, her nipples standing out proud and hard. Ramon kissed the back of her neck and his fingers parted the short hair where her birthmark was. "Check it out."

"Yes, the heart. Perfect," Evan said as he looked at it, then helped Ramon move her to a wide, low bed against one cinderblock wall. They propped up a pile of pillows, and then lay her facedown over them so that her ass was in the air.

"What's a meld?" Wren asked. "Do my hands really have to be tied for this?"

Abby was there by her head. "It'll be really, really good, Wren," she was saying in a low voice. "The most amazing sex ever. It's like the best high in the world. It'll feel better than any sex you've ever had. You'll see God."

"And the future," said Evan from her other side with a chuckle. "I could care less about God. But yes, Wren, we'll keep you tied until we're sure we can trust you."

She felt a pair of clammy hands on her buttocks. "Um, wow," said Steve.

Abby stroked her hair. "Steve's a heart, too, Wren. With you two together, since you're both seers, it'll be amazing. It'll be like the purest love, the purest sex ever."

But then she heard Evan's voice in her mind. *Your sister is so very refreshing. I think that's what attracted me to her in the first place. I'm just going to have Steve fuck your cunt. That is the most powerful of the joinings for sight, and it won't disturb your sister overmuch. But I would so very much love to see every hole of yours filled, Wren. There are three of us here, after all. One of us could take your mouth, while one took your ass, and the third your cunt.*

Wren shivered with desire, the wanton creature that she was in her dreams seeming to come to life in her skin at that moment. But she kept her wits about her. Intellectually speaking, she wanted Steve even less than she had wanted

Evan, and again she thought of Derek, wondering where he was, and if he was still asleep.

She felt their weights shifting on the bed. Someone was touching her clit now. Evan. She could feel him in her mind like a pair of arms holding her. "Ramon, link with me, and read how close to orgasm Steve is. I'll read Wren."

"Hey!" Steve's voice rose in feeble protest. "Evan, does he have to touch me for that? Can't I jerk myself off while he reads me?"

Wren felt a wave of long-suffering tolerance roil through Evan. He felt sorry for Steve, and a touch of affection, but mostly he found him irritating. But he was a good seer and very loyal, if very uptight about sexual things, especially anything that could be deemed homoerotic. "Very well," he acceded. "Ramon, just put a hand on his shoulder to make sure you get a good read."

"Fine with me," Ramon said, and she could feel the mutual disgust between Ramon and Steve. Both of them were *so* very heterosexual.

"The orgasms must be simultaneous for this to work," Evan reminded them. Then they fell silent, as they each began reading whom they needed to.

Wren read them. Abby was thinking she hoped Wren having sex with Steve would be as amazing for her as having sex with Evan was, even though Steve wasn't the same kind of telepath. He was just a seer; he couldn't talk with his mind like Evan could. Nearly all Abby's thoughts were of having sex with Evan, Wren found, as if that one subject had completely taken up her mind.

Evan was thinking about Wren, about how strange it had been to seduce her through dreams, about how he hadn't expected to get so attached, to feel so possessive. But it was *Steve* who had to fuck her for Evan's plans to come to fruition. He had very specific plans of what to do with the information they were about to glean. Wren saw a glimpse of his dreams of riches, of influence. The heart-to-heart meld, seer-to-seer would give him a clear view of market futures and political outcomes that would ensure the future for him and his people.

All Ramon was thinking was, *Thank God I don't have to touch Steve's dick.*

Steve's thoughts were of the stock market, about some very confusing financial stuff Wren couldn't really understand in the state she was in. It was odd, because through it all, she could feel Steve pulsing like a primal ball of lust too. She wondered when he had last had sex, if ever. She delved a little deeper.

Shy. Not many close friends. Trouble with intimacy. A childhood that felt a lot like her own. Hiding his ability while at the same time doubting it was even real. And then meeting Evan and learning it was real and everything changing....

"He's getting close," Ramon said out loud.

Suddenly, Wren knew what she had to do to buy time. She wrapped her own mind around the pulsing ball of need that was Steve and squeezed as hard as she could.

"Oh, fuck! Fuck fuck fuck!" Steve shouted as he came all over his own hand.

The flare of anger from Evan was so hot, Wren cringed from it.

"You moron," Ramon said, shaking his head.

Evan sighed, anger ebbing away and replaced with a spiky irritation. "I suppose we'll have to do this the hard way, then."

Abby sounded angry when she said, "Like this is easy? Evan, this isn't what we discussed."

"Shut up, please, Abby." He ground his teeth in frustration. "I've been trying to respect everyone's needs here, but let's not forget we have a goal, hmm?"

But Wren could feel the secret glee in Evan as he proposed his new plan. "Technically Steve doesn't have to fuck her, though that would be the most powerful way. His flaccid cock in her mouth would be sufficient, and I can make him come at the proper time."

Ramon sounded impressed. "You can? Shit, I didn't know that."

"It's a rare talent, and one I only tend to share with my favorites, like Abby here."

Wren could feel the warmth of his approval sinking through Abby's skin. Her stomach turned a little, both at the thought that Evan was going to make Steve come in her mouth, and that Abby was addicted to him.

God, was Derek addicted to Wren's ability to do that?

Her attention switched quickly back to the present situation, though, as she felt Evan's touch in her mind, as he began to read her.

"I'll make Wren come the old-fashioned way," Evan was saying. But then his voice was there in her mind again. *I've been wanting to fuck you for the longest time. I can make it pleasure like you've never known.*

Pleasure so good I could get addicted to it? Wren answered. *No, thanks.*

Abby told me you were practically a virgin, that you were inexperienced. He was shifting his position, orchestrating the movements of the others to turn Wren over so Steve could get at her mouth, and to spread her legs for him. Ramon rebound her hands above her head, stretched up and tied to the head of the bed somehow.

I was. But I've met someone.

Ahhh. That explains much. Falling in love will make you resistant to the pull of heart-to-heart, seer-to-seer. At least for a little while. If you'd met Steve while you were single, you would have thought you'd found your soul mate.

Then why all the seductive dreams?

To arouse you, to make you mentally ready and emotionally hungry for sex, so that when you met Steve you'd be ripe for the plucking. Ah, I see what you're thinking. You're wondering if you might not have been so attracted to your man if I had not been interfering in your dreams. If that's so, Wren, then maybe you're not so in love with him after all. Maybe it's really me you've been craving all along. She felt the warmth of his breath through her pubic hair.

Her mind rebelled against that idea, that how much she desired Derek was anything but her own will.

Is it such a farfetched idea? I snatched it out of your own head, after all.

Wren wrestled with the thought. Was that why it had felt so right with Derek, why she had been so insatiable? Was it really Evan's doing and not her natural attraction to Derek at all?

What about Abby? Won't she be jealous if you fuck me?

Abby has seen me fuck many women in the club upstairs. After all, that's where I met her. His tongue was warm velvet on her clit, which twitched as she remembered what it felt like to have the silken head of his cock rubbing at that spot.

Yes, but I'm her sister.

And you think this will make a difference to her?

Yes. I'm sure it will.

Because you're the big sister she was always jealous of?

I suppose so.

Perhaps that's because you're worthy of envy, Wren. You're far superior to her in so many ways.

Except I'm not.

You're wrong. You're exceptional and it only makes me want you even more. He slipped a finger into her as he pulled back his tongue and sucked on her clit. *I'm not a heart like Steve. I'm a diamond, and a diamond's soul mate is a rare gem indeed.*

I'm resisting you, she said. *That's the only reason you want me so badly.*

Your body doesn't seem to be resisting.

Wren tried to pull her knees together, but her ankles had been bound toward the corners of the bed. *Damn it, I don't want you, Evan.*

You know you cannot lie with your mind, right?

I don't! But even as she thought it, she could see it was a lie. She wanted Evan at a level deeper than thought. She didn't want to want him, but she did. She wanted to break free of the cocoon she had been in all her life, to be as free as the butterfly, set free by desire, cut loose by the knife of his cock.

And yet. *Well, I don't want to meld with Steve, whatever that is.*

The meld will not hurt you, Wren. It'll feel good. You'll see incredible things. Your power is real. I can teach you how to use it.

But Wren tried to shove away the seductive thought. *You're still getting off on the fact that I'm trying to push you away.*

You are right. When my mind is this open, I cannot hide it. You have unmasked me. The more you fight, the more you reject the idea that I am going to take you, the harder I become, the more electrifying it will be when I finally penetrate you. But you must not think ill of me for it. No man, not even one with iron will, could resist you like this. "Steve."

The man straddled her chest and with her eyes closed, Wren felt something cold and slimy against her lips. His cock, still spunky from having come. She spat and turned her head.

Come now, Wren. Steve's an innocent like you. I promised him a soul mate in you. I had no idea you'd met someone and, as it is, if things don't work out with your man, you might yet find yourself helplessly drawn to Steve. That will make me insanely jealous, but he has been loyal. It would be your choice.

She opened her mouth reluctantly and Steve pushed his cock in, squishy and soft and bitter with come.

My choice, you say? If I do this for you, this meld, and you get what you want, will you leave me alone after that? Wren's hips bucked as his finger slid into her again. *Will you promise to take care of Abby?*

Wren, you are in no position to bargain with me. You already know I am getting off on your reluctance. Don't give me a reason to force you.

What would it be worth to you? For you to promise to take care of Abby, and for you not to fuck me. I'll do this meld for you, and what else?

You are a persistent one. Trying to save yourself for your boy-friend, is that it? Does it feel disloyal to fuck me and to know how much you'll enjoy it?

Yes, yes, it does. It wasn't really possible to lie about that, either. This was her dream lover, after all, pushing her closer and closer to orgasm, each press of his finger into her making her moan and her lower half convulse.

I'll tell you what I'll do then, Wren. I'll respect your wish to leave your cunt alone, but I'll take your ass instead. You'll meld with Steve. I make no promises about Abby. She's her own woman, and our relationship is not for you to judge.

You self-righteous asshole. Then she gasped as he shifted his mouth lower and began to tease at her anus with the tip of his tongue. *It's a deal.*

Very good. Now, remember that you agreed to this. If you be-come so fixated on anal pleasure after this that you can never get the smell of shit out of his sheets, it will be your own fault and not mine.

The next thing she felt was his finger, but it was chilled and slimy as it penetrated her asshole. He was using some kind of lube. He pulled out and came back again, with more of the cold, slippery, stuff. Wren had never, ever touched her-self there and was surprised to find it similar to being pen-etrated vaginally. It was different, and yet it wasn't. As he began to piston his fingers in and out of her, accustoming her to the sensation, she gasped. It felt good.

I told you. It's all sex. Any part of me penetrating any part of you. It will all feel good.

Steve's penis in my mouth isn't very sexy and doesn't feel par-ticularly good.

Another sign that perhaps, despite you both being hearts, you may not be that compatible. Whereas you and I...can you feel that heat? That spark?

Indeed, each time his fingers—two of them together now—curved into her, she felt sparks of desire shoot from her center to her extremities.

Maybe we are meant for each other, Wren.

Her only answer was a moan as the fingers inside her felt more and more as if they were stroking her clit. So strange, but her clit was definitely swollen as if it were being touched. She supposed perhaps it was being touched from the other side.

Evan made a low, hungry sound, like some predator with his jaws around his prey. *You are incredible. I think you might be able to come just from this. Let's see how you feel with my cock instead.*

Wren couldn't help it. She held her breath, as the blunt, spongy head of Evan's cock rubbed against her pucker. Impossibly large, there was no way it could fit....

She cried out as it breached her, the pain a strange, dull one that only made her clit throb harder. Then as he moved, seating himself deeper, the pain disappeared entirely, replaced with an even stranger sense of completion.

Wren opened her eyes and looked up at Steve. His head was tilted back, and Evan's hands were on his shoulders.

Suck him a bit, Wren. I assure you he'll be more palatable if he's hard.

She moved her tongue, her lips, fellating him until she felt it stirring, blood rushing hot to the organ, and a salty ooze of pre-come slicked her tongue.

That's it. Be loving.

Steve moaned above her. In his head, she could see he was sinking into a kind of trance, the visions of numbers and stock symbols sharpening.

I know I'm far from the world's most virtuous man, Evan thought, *but I do try to love those around me. Don't be afraid to love, Wren. Too many people with our gifts are. They have sensed or experienced too much of the negative emotions in the world, leaving them too scarred to love. We belong among our own kind.*

Wren's own thoughts were no longer as coherent as words, but she could grasp the grandeur of his dream. This was just the first step to building a haven for telepaths. They needed money, and influence, real estate, and freedom...and Evan's cock moving inside her was an overwhelming sensory experience. It was stimulation like she'd never known. Were her own powers being driven to new heights as her arousal was? The hard flesh parting hers seemed to push at things inside her, in her heart, in her head, nerves all over her body firing and glowing.

She imagined it was Derek, then, that it was Derek's cock plunging into her, Derek's hands that gripped her hipbones so hard it was going to leave a bruise. *Derek, Derek, Derek....*

Oh, you fucking bitch! She could feel how wounded Evan felt, that she was imagining another man. He fucked her harder, pouring his anger into each thrust, but it just felt better and better, pushing her higher and higher.

As the orgasm hit her, the bitter flood of Steve's come coated her tongue and she gagged, coughing and choking, but it seemed like it was happening very far away. She felt hands lifting her, moving her, the star of Steve's orgasm burning bright in her mind.

Derek. She could see him in the parking lot, talking with someone else, a man...someone...but the moment she touched his mind, his words died away.

Wren!

I'm here. I'm in the basement of the club. Abby's here, too.

She felt him put his hand on the roof of the SUV, as lust, sudden and consuming, swept through him. She could feel the pulse of his blood in his cock, as he went from flaccid to straining in a matter of heartbeats. *Wren, are you being held captive?*

Not really. I think they'll let me go after this. Then an aftershock of orgasm hit her, and drew her attention back to her body. She was sitting up now, Ramon behind her, hands cupping her breasts, while Steve lapped at her clit. And Evan was on the bed, Abby writhing under him, as he thrust so hard Abby's head nearly hit the headboard behind them. *Derek...I need you.*

God, Wren. You...you make me feel...

I know. Wait a moment...

She let herself go, another orgasm shaking her, even as she used the peak of her power to plunder her sister's mind, to answer the questions crowding her own thoughts.

Oh, shit, that's what I was afraid of. She pushed the knowledge at Derek without words, that the club was run by a telepath. Since he needed sex to trigger his powers, a sex club was a useful front. But some women got addicted to sex with him. Abby had been one of them, and she was still functional. But there were others who were not so lucky, who basically lay in a haze of lust day after day. They kept them hidden, locked away in another part of the cellar. Only Evan and Abby knew the truth about them and otherwise they really didn't know what to do other than to keep them hidden. Only the promise that Evan would come and "feed" them would convince them to eat.

Helena Riggs was one of them. She'd had to be restrained after she had masturbated so much she'd damaged herself....

Wren! I'm coming for you.

No! Derek, call the police! I'll be okay!

But her connection to his thoughts went fuzzy, as if his emotions overwhelmed reason. Anger, hurt, jealousy, rage, protectiveness, fear...she felt all of these things tangle in him before she lost her hold.

Her attention returned to the people around her. Evan was still fucking Abby hard, and Abby cried out and clung to him in what was obviously the throes of orgasm. As she went limp, he kept on, though, pushing and pushing. Abby convulsed suddenly, crying out again in surprise, and Wren knew he was making her come with his mind.

But still, he had not come himself. Wren wondered how many times Abby had come while Wren had not been paying attention.

"Oh, God, Evan..." Abby could barely choke out the words. Wren listened for her thoughts. *I don't think I can take another one.*

But you will, won't you, my sweet? You wouldn't want to leave me unsatisfied, would you? That would be far from fair.

But Evan, God... I don't know if I can.

You can. The last time I fucked you with fewer than twelve orgasms, you complained it hadn't been enough for you.

I just want you to come, Abby pleaded. *I need to feel you come with me! Don't make me come again if you're not there yet.*

Ah, but that is the trouble, my sweet. I am trying. Between Helena and you and the others, it takes a greater and greater extreme of sensation to get me off.

Abby reached up then and pinched his nipples hard. Evan responded with a growl, throwing her into the throes of orgasm again. It seemed to Wren that this one went on longer than the others, and at the end of it, Abby's mouth was slack, her eyes rolled up in her head.

Wren kicked at Steve, forcing him to move his head as she put one hand on Evan, one on Abby, and *pushed.* But as she did, Steve slid his fingers inside her, and quite suddenly, all five of them were coming, Ramon in hot spurts against her back, Evan and Abby together, and Steve with a surprised bellow, only a tiny issue coming from his cock after three orgasms in such a short interval.

And Wren herself was flung out of her body entirely, floating above the scene.

Evan recovered himself first. "Well," he said, as he gestured to the others to rouse themselves and help him move the unconscious Abby, and Wren, too. "That was certainly a surprise. It seems there's more to Wren Delacourt than just being a seer."

"Oh, shit," Steve said. "Do you think she was reading us, too?"

Evan clucked his tongue. "And if she was? Steve, you know we have nothing to hide. I plan to tell her of my goals to create a safe haven for people like us as soon as she wakes. Now if you and Ramon could help move them, I'd be grateful. Put Abby in her room. Ramon, put Wren in my bed for now, and then send one of the girls to clean up down here."

She followed her body, as Ramon carried her easily through a doorway, down a hall, through a heavier door, and eventually into another room. This was clearly where Evan lived. There was laundry on the floor near a basket, books scattered over the side table, a clothes dresser covered with knickknacks. The small lamp on the bedside table was the only light.

She looked down at herself, naked, debauched, her thighs sticky. Her lips were swollen. Ramon threw a blanket over her and left.

Out-of-body experiences were one of those things she'd heard about but never experienced. She wracked her brain trying to recall if she'd ever heard a story that included how the experience ended. She tried to touch herself, but she didn't really have arms to reach with—those were on her body.

Duh. I should have guessed that.

Wren was a bit worried to just leave her body there, but she had to know what was happening to Derek. Was he upstairs trying to argue his way in? Or just fight his way in? Her last glimpse of his mind had shown such turmoil.

Could she even drift away from her body, direct her movements as a spirit, or whatever she was? She tried to feel for Derek again, but her body was utterly sated and her power was weak.

But she could move. Her consciousness floated up through the floor and she found herself in the women's dressing room. There was Suzanne, looking at herself in the mirror and chatting with another woman there. They were both wearing something that looked like circus costumes, with feathers on their heads and...oh. Wren finally figured

166 × CECILIA TAN

out they were dressed like circus ponies, with small saddles on and reins trailing down each of their backs.

She moved through the doors into the lounge area. Derek! He was in his cowboy outfit and he was talking with Bob, who was in a lion tamer's getup. Their heads were leaning close together. She could not hear what they were saying because she didn't have ears. She focused on Derek. Couldn't she read him if she really tried?

The next thing she knew, she was looking at Bob's serious expression through Derek's eyes. And she could hear what they were saying. "I understand your worry. If she came here alone and now you don't see her, it's natural to worry. You said you talked to her, though?"

"Well, she called me," Derek said, a little white lie since she hadn't "called" him using her cell phone. "But we got cut off. She was telling me she was okay, but that she thought there might be women who were here against their will. She was trying to tell me something about addicts."

Bob shook his head. "I haven't seen any hint of junkies around here, but if they hide it real well...I don't know, Derek. They seem to run a nice, clean club, and I'd hate to see it busted up by the police over a misunderstanding or a miscommunication, you know? If they're, like, drugging women into being prostitutes or something, more power to you if you break that kind of thing up, but...."

"Yeah, I know." Derek shifted uneasily. "She just sounded upset, you know? And then we got cut off."

"Well, it's a good thing we brought Charlene with us tonight so we could get you in. I think we ought to have a look around and see what we can see. Maybe you'll meet up with Wren and find out everything's okay after all."

Derek swallowed his skepticism. There was so much he couldn't tell Bob, and that weighed on him. He scanned the room, which was much more crowded than the previous week. Lots of people had chosen gladiator and serving-girl kinds of costumes, along with a latex-clad nurse, and one Tarzan and Jane. "All right. We'll have a look around, but if I find anything wrong, just so you know, I'm calling the police."

The two men moved to greet Suzanne and Charlene then, and Wren felt a surge of jealousy as Derek put his arm loosely around Charlene's shoulders. The group made their way into the next room, but the dancer on the stage didn't hold Derek's interest even a little, and Charlene happily trotted ahead of him as he held onto her reins.

The next room already had people in it. Derek was trying not to stare, but the walls were lined with beds like a hospital ward, and there were couples fucking on about half of them. Wren wondered if it were Derek's thought or her own: *God, that man's ass is hairy.*

"What's beyond this room?" Derek whispered to Charlene.

"Come on, it gets kinky after this," she whispered back. She led the way through another door, this one also painted with the vine motif, but with more leaves and the flower at the top was beginning to open. The next room had what looked like a gynecologist's table, a massage table, and some other odd platforms in it, with one couple already at play. The male partner had laid out an assortment of dildos and things alongside the exam table, and several of them were glistening wet. Two other couples were watching as he moved his arm, clearly pistoning back and forth in an unmistakable

168 × CECILIA TAN

motion. Derek drifted closer and Wren shared his shock as he realized the man's entire hand had gone into her. His wrist disappeared where her body began.

God, you see? Surely your cock isn't that big, Wren said inside his head. *And I'm not made of glass!*

He gave no indication he had heard.

There were two more doors, one that Charlene indicated went to the women-only area, and the final one, where the flower on the door had fully bloomed.

They went through to find the room painted mostly black. Here there were no beds, but there were what looked like medieval torture racks, and the massage table had ropes tied to its legs. The room was empty.

"You have to bring your own whips and chains," Charlene explained, "if you're into that sort of thing."

"Er, I'm not," Derek said. "Just curious. Thanks for taking me through here."

They went back to the room where the man was fisting his partner. She was whooping with joy— shouting "oh yeah!"— and Wren could feel Derek couldn't hold back a grin. He looked at the door to the women-only space.

"You think anyone's in there?" he asked Charlene in a whisper.

"Dunno, you want to see? I'll look first." She giggled and slipped into the room. A moment later she came back out. "Nope, clear as a whistle."

His grin got wider. Everyone's attention was riveted on the woman and her husband, even the one woman who was corseted like an employee.

"I'll just take a peek," he whispered. "You watch the show here, and if I get caught, you won't get in trouble."

Wren's jealousy spiked again when the woman's answer was to stroke a hand along his cheek with an "aw shucks" expression on her face.

But then Derek was on the move. He was thinking that the women-only room probably had a door on its far wall that would possibly connect up with the stage door that the dancer had entered through back in that very first room after the lounge.

He walked quickly through the mostly pink- and yellow-colored room, the sheets thrown over the couches in here done in bright flowered patterns. Yes, there was a curtain, and behind it, a door. He went through it and found himself in a dimly lit service hallway. Wren recognized it and it seemed as she got more excited, so did he. She urged him to find the stairs down. Soon, he had made his way down to the room where "the orgy"—as Wren now thought of it—had taken place.

He ducked under the stairs suddenly as voices came into earshot.

"Honestly, Ramon, I don't know. I have no doubt you're a spade, but something's blocking you from letting loose your power."

"It's just scary, you know? I don't want to hurt anybody."

"You won't. Your ability would only be used to protect those important to us—you know that, right?"

"It's still scary...."

"I know."

Their voices faded as they went up the stairs, and Wren could feel Derek putting the facts together. Was Councilman Riggs considered a threat to them? Was that why he was in a coma now?

Wren tried to remember where her body was lying, tried to lead him toward it. Yes, through the heavy door, it was beyond that.

But Derek's attention was drawn by a door along the hall that had a padlock on the outside. It was a fairly normal-looking door, but the padlock and hasp had clearly been added later, the screws and latch not quite fitting the door frame and the hasp bent so that the lock would fit. There was light coming from under the door. Why would a locked store room have a light on?

His heart hammered as he thought about what Wren had told him. Could Mrs. Riggs be behind this door?

He knocked on the door. "Hello?"

A female voice was suddenly close by the door, a hand rattling the knob. "Evan? Is that you?"

"Helena Riggs?" Derek called.

"Oh my God, yes, who are you? Ramon? What's going on? Evan said he was going to come and see me tonight, but he hasn't been by." She rattled the doorknob again.

"Um, please just hang tight, Helena," he said, wondering if it was a good idea to try to let her out, or if Stockholm syndrome would complicate matters too much. It might just be best to let the police find her like this. She might still argue that it was all a kinky sex game, she wasn't really "kidnapped."

Derek leaned against the door frame, considering. What if it really was all a kinky sex game? It wasn't a police matter if a woman left her husband for something more exciting. But if the relationship was truly abusive? Addictive? Derek couldn't imagine a relationship where being locked in a room all the time was desirable. But he'd seen the "dungeon" upstairs, and clearly there were things he didn't fathom.

Wren tugged frantically at him, trying to get him to move. She was so close to him now, she wanted him to find her.

His feet finally moved as he realized he might have limited time before he was discovered. He tried the next door down, which was not locked from the outside.

Nor from the inside. He was startled to find a woman lying on a bed on top of the bedspread as if someone else had laid her there. *That's Abby!* Wren tried to tell him, but once again it didn't seem he had heard. A quick glance made it look as if she was living in the room, clothes hanging on a rack, books piled by the bed, a poster of a Dali landscape taped to the wall above the bed. She stirred and sat up.

Recognition washed through him like a swallow of wine. This was either Abby or the woman he'd seen that had made him think she was here. "Abby Delacourt?"

"Yeah," she said tiredly. "Who the hell are you?"

"I'm your sister's boyfriend," he said without hesitation. With conviction and passion. Suddenly Wren felt as if she were spinning. "She's been worried sick about you."

Abby's face crumpled with guilt. "Oh God. I would have called her, but Evan wanted to try to get her and Steve together, and I would have just messed that up. And Evan doesn't like me going out too much."

Derek waved a hand. "Do you know where Wren is? I'm here to get her out. If you want to stay, that's up to you."

Abby's guilty look only deepened. "Um, she's probably around here somewhere." She stood up and pulled on a robe, blushing a little. "Come on."

Abby led him to Evan's door. She knocked. "Evan, you in there?"

He's not here! Only I'm here! God, this out-of-body stuff was frustrating.

Abby turned the knob and the door opened easily. Her voice dropped to a whisper. "Here she is."

Derek hurried to Wren's side. Abby shifted from foot to foot. "I'll just leave you two alone, how about that?" she said hurriedly, then fled, closing the door behind her. A rattling sound drew Derek's attention, though, and he hurried to the door only to find it locked from the outside.

Chapter Ten

DEREK CURSED and flung himself hard at the door, but this lock wasn't quite as flimsy as the one on Mrs. Riggs's door. He cursed again and rubbed his shoulder.

Wren pulsed with urgency and Derek turned suddenly to look at her. "Wren?" He touched his temple.

Yes! I'm here! I'm just...disconnected!

But he didn't seem to be able to hear her words. Just sense her presence. He went back to the bed and cupped her cheek. "Wren, wake up."

She could feel his hand, warm and solid, and yet she was still hovering over the bed, looking down at them. *Kiss me, Derek, kiss me, please. Surely that's all I'll need to wake up....*

He lifted his head, as if he could almost hear her. He brushed his thumb over her lips.

Yes!

"Wren, are you in there?" he whispered. She could feel the apprehension rising in him, wondering if the same thing had happened to her as happened to Councilman Riggs.

No, no, no. I'm right here.

His fear subsided and he looked at her, puzzled. "I can feel you're here. But it's not like when I can hear you."

Yes, yes.

"Do you...do you want me to kiss you? I have this urge to kiss you."

Yes!

"I feel...I feel this sense of rightness about it." He leaned over and brushed his lips over hers. Electricity seemed to tingle all through her at that.

More, more....

"I think I should try to get us out of here, Wren. I should try that door again."

No! Stay with me.

He touched his forehead. "Okay, you don't like that idea. I get it. Let me at least call the police. These people could be dangerous. Your own sister locked us in here."

She relented. Calling the police was probably an excellent idea. She radiated impatient approval. Derek made the call quickly and then returned his attention to her. "I hope that doesn't get Suzanne and Bob into too much trouble," he said. "Hopefully they took my disappearance as a sign they should clear out."

Well, if we could wake me up, I could warn them, Wren thought.

"I have a feeling you want me to kiss you again."

Oh, yes. Yesyesyes.

He let out a breath, and she could feel him trying to let go of fear and the ball of rage that kept trying to burn its way out when he saw that she was naked under the blanket. "Jesus, Wren...."

Kiss me. Touch me. I need you.

His fingertips traced the curve of her cheek, and he brushed his lips over hers again. Oh, that felt so good. Something she could actually feel.

More, harder.

He shook his head. "It feels right, and yet, I know it's wrong...."

It's right. Derek, I need you!

Her urgency spiked and he gasped, his eyes falling closed as he felt it wash through him. "Oh, God, Wren...."

Her need only intensified as she saw his trousers starting to tent.

More.

"All right," he whispered, thinking maybe arousing her would do the trick. It seemed to be what triggered and strengthened her abilities, after all. His fingertips ran down her neck, and he kissed in a line following the curve down to her shoulder. He slipped the blanket down and continued his march of kisses, down her bosom until he reached one petal-soft nipple. He drew it into his mouth, flicking it with a gentle tongue tip, then sucking as it hardened.

Wren's body stirred slightly against him. *Oh, yes, good, more, more....*

He rolled her onto her back and continued his exploration of her skin with his mouth. He traversed the valley between her two breasts, then brought the other nipple to match the first, licking the hard bud again and again.

Wren felt a burst of lust. That was exactly the way he had licked her clit, and she could feel the thought forming in his head that he wanted to do so again.

God, yes, Derek. Now....

His hand slid over her pubic hair, cupping her and massaging gently until he felt her body move again, just slightly, against him. Then he moved down the bed, parting her knees inch by inch and moving one foot aside, until he could lie on his belly between her legs. He parted her lips with his fingers, then circled her clit with just the tip of his index finger.

Oh, yes. Oh, God, Derek, please....

Wren! I can hear you!

Good good good...I need you want you need you....

All right, sweetheart. I'm here. I'm here. He lowered his mouth to her clit and sucked it softly, flicking his tongue and then grazing the flesh with his teeth. Wren felt herself being drawn closer, but she was still looking down on them, rather than looking from behind her own eyes.

I'm so empty, Derek....

He made soothing noises with his throat, as he slipped a finger inside her and slowly drew it in and out. *How's that? Does that feel good?*

Yesyesyes....

He returned to sucking her clit while finger-fucking her, and Wren felt her arousal mounting. Perhaps if she came, she'd return to her body? But how could she *come* if she wasn't *there*?

More!

He slipped a second finger in alongside the first. Wren flooded him with her need.

God, you're so wet, so slick.

All for you. She couldn't stop the thought from forming that she'd kept Evan from fucking her there, to save herself for Derek. She felt the curl of his anger, aimed not at her, but at the men who had used her, rising like a skirl of smoke. *I need you now more than ever.*

He could hardly get his pants off fast enough. Rational thought was shredding away, as she filled his mind with images of the orgy and how much she longed for him, then and now. How she'd saved herself for him.

Don't make me wait anymore!

I won't. He settled himself between her legs, suckling one nipple again while his hand strayed across the other. She could feel the threads of fear, reaching up out of the dark swamp of his memories, trying to pull him back down, but their grasp was feeble in comparison to the more immediate emotions that gripped him. How dare they? And how he'd failed her by waiting this long. No more waiting. She needed him.

There was not enough spare thought to consider a condom or any more trivialities. The reality of his cock head pulsing against her clit, where it lay nestled, was far too overwhelming. Animal instinct told him to shift his weight, to press it just *there....*

Wren's body responded, moving against him, driving herself onto him an inch or two—the ache of being empty far worse than the pain of entry. He shuddered, trying to hold back for just a moment more, but it was only a moment, and then his hips answered hers with a thrust of their own and he was inside her, fully inside.

"Derek!" She had a voice! And arms with which she clung to him, wrapping her legs around him, too. "Oh, Derek...."

His answer was a low sound in his throat and a new thrust, drawing back and filling her again.

She cried out in ecstasy as she felt him move inside her, felt their bodies as connected as their minds in a rhythm so ancient she felt as if it echoed every sound in nature, the trees swaying in the wind, the waves lapping at the lake shore.

The ticking of a broken clock, where the pendulum swung but time never moved forward, cycling around and around—she had no sense of time moving forward. Even her breath, her heartbeat, seemed synchronized to the plunge of his cock into her, the head touching her in a way she'd never been touched before. She'd had a few partners with whom she'd tried intercourse, but none of them had struck sparks of pleasure with each thrust. The head of his cock was like a match, striking the flint inside her over and over.

With a sudden cry she caught fire, orgasm exploding through her every nerve. Her consciousness expanded suddenly then, like a star gone supernova, and she could see and hear and feel everyone in the building, in the parking lot outside, in the cars going by....

The police were on the way. She only gripped Derek more tightly, urging him to fuck harder, wanting more still. She could see Suzanne lounging with her husband and the woman they had brought with them, sated and happy. Wren wasn't sure if she could hear it, but she tried to send a warning, an urgency to leave, an image of the police—and saw Suzanne stand quickly, hurrying the others.

But Wren's attention was being pulled back to Derek, to the rising tide in him, to the electricity that seemed to be building in his flesh as his pace increased.

"Harder," she whispered, wanting one more explosion for herself, and craving his too. She could push, she knew, she could push her mind through his and send them both spinning instantly into release, but she would not. Locking her legs around his, she rocked against him, her body meeting his again and again.

A sudden thought struck her—that he wasn't wearing protection—and felt the echo of the thought in his own mind in the split second he tried to pull away, but she held him fast. She wasn't sure where the knowledge came from, if it was something that Evan could have planted in her mind, or if the experience had opened the instinctive knowledge of her mind and body she had missed before, but she reached into herself and knew she was not ready to conceive. He felt what she felt, knew what she knew, and redoubled his efforts to make her come with his cock.

Wren wasn't sure what sent her over the edge more, the feeling of him inside her, touching her just the right way, or the feeling of him holding himself back, straining against his own body's inevitability to make sure she reached another peak.

Maybe both. This time, her orgasm mingled with his, and instead of an explosive outward expansion, her mind fused even more strongly with his, anchoring them to each other in a spinning coil of energy that only gradually slowed to a stop.

Then she looked at him, at a bit of hair plastered to his forehead damp with sweat, his mouth slightly open in incredulity and his eyes dazed but alight with joy. She craned upward and kissed him and he trembled softly against her, lowering his full weight bit by bit. She could still feel throbbing inside her and she squeezed the cock still inside her. He lifted himself again so that they looked into each other's eyes, and he pulled back for another gentle thrust.

"Oh!" He was softening slowly, and was still hard enough to give her more. She bit her lip but did not look away from his eyes as he fucked her gently now, with no more thought of orgasm, only enjoying being joined and the milder but no less pleasurable sensation of it. Three, four, five thrusts, a melting sort of pleasure seeming to spread from her core, from him, from between her legs out to the tips of her fingers and toes. "Oh, yes...."

"Wren." He seemed unable to say anything more, but perhaps he did not have to. Her name communicated everything to her. His love, his amazement, his admiration, his care, his protectiveness, his desire to be with her in every sense of the word.

She kissed him again, and at last he was too soft to stay inside her any longer. He slipped out and then slid to his side, pulling her with him and cradling her in his arms. "Wren."

She just nodded in response, pressing kisses to his damp skin. Now, oh, she wanted to sleep. To just sleep in his arms.

But she could not quite forget that they were locked in Evan's bedroom, and that the police were on the way. "We should get up and get dressed," she murmured.

He made a hum of agreement, but did not move for a few seconds, as reluctant to let go of her as she was to let go of him. A brief hiss made her sit up, though.

Someone had just slid a piece of paper under the door.

* * * *

Wren found herself shivering where she sat in a chair in a hallway at the police station. She hugged herself and wished she could make the air around her warmer. "Darn," she said, rubbing her forehead. "That would have been a handy talent."

She was wearing some mismatched clothes of Evan's, which she'd figured he wouldn't be needing, seeing as he had fled the scene before the police had arrived.

Wren had warned him herself, without meaning to, when she'd tried to warn Bob and Suzanne.

She took out Abby's note and looked at it again. She could make out Derek's voice and the detective he was talking to, but not their individual words. If she let herself go, almost half asleep, she could sense what they were saying, but she was afraid to slip too far into the trance state. The technique Derek had used to pin her to her own body earlier would probably be considered rude to perform in the middle of the station.

She read the note instead.

Dear Wren,

I'm so so so so so sorry things didn't work out here. I got wrapped up in stuff and I didn't even realize what day it was until the day came.

Wren assumed she meant the anniversary of their parents' death.

I'd already promised Evan I'd do something and, well, that's when I realized maybe it was time I start loving the people around me more than the ones who have already departed.

She felt a little ill, wondering how much of Abby's feelings were truly love, and which were manipulated and orchestrated by Evan, both through her mind and with his actions and words. She was quite sure Abby was sincere, but the premise still felt rotten.

I never thought you'd be so worried about me that you'd come looking for me. I really thought Steve was going to be the guy for you finally, after what Evan had said. I was only thinking of you when I decided to stay out of the way, because I knew if I introduced him to you, you'd hate him instantly. I thought you'd connect with him right away, and then I'd be able to see you all the time once you joined our family.

It didn't seem to occur to Abby that she and Wren were already family. "If that was your way of showing you loved me, you sure picked a weird way of doing it," she said to the paper in her hand.

Thank you for the warning. Evan and I are going to disappear with Ramon and Steve and a few others. Don't look for me. I won't contact you because I don't want trouble with the police and Evan says they'll use you to try to find us. Maybe when it all blows over in a year or two. And I'm so sorry for locking you and your boyfriend up. He seems really nice! I just didn't know what Evan was going to say about him snooping around.

Wren shook her head. She had little doubt that if he could justify it somehow, Evan would have kept her caged up like Mrs. Riggs. She was somewhere here, too, giving a statement to the police. Wren had caught a glimpse of her, haggard and wan but her head held high.

I wish I could tell you more about Evan and how much he's changed me. I never thought I would find a love like this—it's so far beyond anything I ever experienced before. Looks like you're going through the same thing! I wish we could sit and talk and you could tell me all about him, too. Maybe someday.

Love, Abby

"Ms. Delacourt?"

She looked up from the note to see a uniformed officer standing there with a cup of coffee in a paper cup. He was trying to hand it to her.

"I thought you might want this to warm you up. You look cold."

She cradled it in her hands, grateful for the warmth both in the cup and in his smile. "Thank you. That was thoughtful of you."

He shrugged. "Derek's a good guy. I knew him at school. I'm Mark Hammond."

"Nice to meet you." She shook his hand and realized as they touched that she got a whisper of his inner state. He wasn't being guarded around her, she realized. He was hoping everything would turn out well.

Derek and the detective came out of the room. Wren couldn't remember this one's name now; she was too tired. A different one had taken a statement from her earlier. She yawned.

"If you want," Derek was saying to the detective, "I could drop Mrs. Riggs off at home. Her house is only a few doors down from mine."

"Ah," the man said, as if that explained a lot to him. He rubbed his eyes. "I could take her to the hospital. They wouldn't turn her away from her husband's bedside."

Derek put a hand on the detective's shoulder. "Or I could take her to the hospital, and you could get on tracking the fugitives, eh, Susser?"

"We're already doing that." Detective Susser's weariness seemed to recede as he focused on the crime. "Thank God Mrs. Riggs is going to press charges. If we had to wait for some ADA to decide whether to pursue a case, forget it. Go on, take the ladies home."

The next thing Wren knew, she was handing the coffee back to Mark, Mrs. Riggs had appeared from somewhere, and all three of them were getting into Derek's SUV.

He waited until the engine had warmed up and he was making his way out of the parking lot to say, "I'm glad I took Diana's advice when I started up. She's the one who told me to cultivate a good relationship with the police."

"Mark said he went to school with you," Wren said.

"Yeah, that helped a lot. And I managed to help out Susser with some things a few years ago, so there you go." He turned to Mrs. Riggs in the passenger seat. "Helena, it's your choice. The hospital or home?"

Wren could feel her debating, and she blinked. Her telepathy seemed to be flickering on and off, even though now she wasn't the slightest bit aroused. There were a million questions she wanted to ask Evan, but he was gone.

Maybe the police would find him. She patted the bulk in the pocket of her borrowed coat, wondering when she would get a chance to look at it.

"The hospital," Mrs. Riggs finally said. She had short waves of golden hair, frosted with silver, and seemed to glow in the street lights. "I don't know what you told the police, but I'm quite certain Evan or one of his men were behind it. But how can it be proven? A psychic attack doesn't leave evidence."

Derek nodded while Wren listened avidly to see if she would reveal any more of what she knew of Evan's abilities. But the woman fell silent.

Wren fell into a doze then, or perhaps a daze. She was aware of the SUV moving, but not of time passing, and she felt Helena Riggs's guilt spike as they pulled into the hospital parking lot.

Wren followed them into the hospital, Derek supporting Mrs. Riggs with his arm. A cop was there to meet them. Wren was vaguely aware that Detective Susser had arranged it, and soon they were all inside the councilman's room. The cop went to stand outside.

Mrs. Riggs put a hand to her mouth as if she were holding back tears, and Derek put his arm around Wren as if to steer her out of the room, too.

"Wait!" Wren's eyes went wide. "He's here."

She could almost see him, hovering over his own body, frustrated and frantic.

Mrs. Riggs turned to her. "Can you talk to him? What's happened to him?"

Wren closed her eyes. He was there, yet she couldn't seem to reach him, just as when she had been out of body, she hadn't been able to reach anyone directly. "Try...try holding his hand."

Mrs. Riggs did so without hesitation. Wren could feel the disconnected spirit drawn closer, as if Mrs. Riggs were the battery fueling the electromagnet.

Wren nodded. "That brought him closer to his body. He's just... having trouble getting back in."

"You can see that?"

"See...feel...it's hard to say which sense I'm using," Wren said. "But it happened to me before. I think it was an accident with me. I couldn't say with your husband."

"How did you get back in?" Mrs. Riggs squeezed her husband's hand tight, possibly tight enough to cause pain, but Wren saw him sinking even lower, blanketing his body, but not yet inside.

Wren glanced at Derek and saw he was blushing and not about to say anything. Wren answered, "Well, Derek, um, kissed me."

To her surprise, Mrs. Riggs smiled, a sparkle of tears in her eyes. "Like a fairy tale." And before Wren could explain or make a move to leave them in privacy, the woman had turned to grasp her husband by the cheeks and press a full kiss to his mouth.

"Oh, thank God," Derek said in relief for more reasons than one when Jim Riggs opened his eyes.

"Helena," he rasped.

She kissed him again and dissolved into tears.

* * * *

Derek's house was closer to the hospital than Wren's, which was as good a reason as any to head there. They'd have to retrieve Wren's car from behind the club tomorrow. Now, all she could think of was sleep.

She undressed completely as soon as they were in the bedroom, and she dug through Derek's closet for the softest old oxford shirt she could find. She put it on for a nightshirt and soon they were brushing their teeth together in the master bathroom.

Then they climbed into bed, and nestled into each other's arms.

They lay quietly for a while, and Wren found herself now almost too tired to sleep. "I have a confession to make," she said quietly, listening to his heart beat with one ear against his chest.

"Oh?" He sounded bemused.

"I figure I better tell you, since the next time we make love you'll probably find out anyway." She said it jokingly, though she knew it was quite possibly true. "I stole something from the crime scene."

"You mean besides those clothes of his you took?"

She nodded. "I took his diary."

"Wren." His voice held a note of uncertainty.

"I don't know if it'll help me or not. But he knew a lot more about telepathic abilities than I do. He made it sound as if there was a lot to know, beyond just his own experience. I only glanced at it while you were getting dressed."

He silenced her with a kiss, then spoke. "Well, if you find anything in there that might hint where they went, it could come in handy."

And despite how well she knew him, despite having been melded to his thoughts mere hours ago, Wren discovered he could still surprise her. "You mean, we might go find them?"

"Maybe," he demurred. "Helena Riggs wants to press kidnapping charges. I don't think we should deprive the police of their fun. But I thought you might want to try one more time to get your sister out of there."

Wren sighed. "It's useless if she doesn't want to go. But maybe she'll see the light about Evan. Who knows? If she's pissed enough at him when she leaves, she might go tell the police herself."

188 × CECILIA TAN

She felt his grip squeeze her tighter. "If she planned to do something like that, don't you think he'd read it in her mind?"

"Oh." Right. Wren shivered even in the warmth of his arms. "But even so. We can't very well just kidnap her ourselves. I think she really does love him."

"Do you think he loves her back?"

She thought back to the orgy, to the jungle of feelings that had tangled all around her. "I think that he thinks that he does. Maybe that means that he does. I'm not sure."

He kissed her softly behind the ear. "Can you tell what I'm thinking now?"

Wren closed her eyes and let him trail kisses down her neck. He should be easy to hear, like finding a familiar channel on the radio dial, a strong, nearby signal.

He whispered it just as she locked on. "I love you, Wren Delacourt."

And I love you. Her hand traveled over the curve of his shoulder, down the planes of his back to the curve of his tailbone. Desire stirred in her and she pressed herself against him.

They say an orgasm can sometimes cure insomnia, he thought. She could feel his cock stiffening against her leg and a low throb settled in her groin.

I want you.

I'm here. He shifted them so that his free hand could probe between her legs, stroking her until she was wet and moaning aloud. He slipped one finger in carefully.

She could not hide the sensation she felt from him, not with thought and feeling flowing so freely between them. She was sore, her so-soft flesh battered by his so-hard cock earlier. And yet the slide of his finger awakened the hunger to have him again. He worked her clit with his thumb and her G-spot with the finger inside her and before long she was spasming against his hand, crying out and demanding more with both voice and mind.

Your wish is my command, he thought as he reached for a condom and lay back to roll it over the stiff flesh.

Before he could climb atop her again, Wren straddled his legs. He could feel the spike of apprehension in him as he had a brief flash of Katy, his first love, looming over him this way, and....

Wren moved into place, using one hand to guide the head of his cock back and forth in the ample wetness between her lips before easing down onto it.

Oh yes, oh God yes. She felt every inch of him as he pressed gradually inside her, the soreness of her flesh transmuting into a sensation of pleasure as he filled her. As she rose and fell in a slow rhythm, she fell into a trance, each thrust like a deep, cleansing breath.

She had no idea how long she fucked him that way, only that it felt good, so very good, her body half asleep but her desire awake—fully awake, perhaps for the first time in her life. She lay atop him, chest to chest, cheek to cheek, and he held her in place and thrust upward into her.

Do you want to come again?

No, she didn't. She wanted him to fuck her to sleep, so she could dream that even while she slept, he was inside her, filling her. *You're my dream lover now.*

Yes, love, for as long as you'll have me.

She closed her eyes and let herself sink deeper into her own flesh, her own mind, as he fucked her just that way, slow and steady, for a heartbeat, then for a minute, then for an hour. At some point he groaned heavily, shuddering against her, cock twitching and spasming deep inside her, then he resumed massaging her inside with his cock. She slipped into true sleep with him still inside.

_____

THE END

Also Available from Red Silk Editions

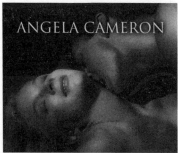

Blood & Sex: Michael
by Angela Cameron

This is a spine-chilling and erotic tale of a Mafia vampire and the detective who is determined to bring to justice a serial killer. Detective Victoria Tyler allows Mafia vampire Michael to "take her neck" and lead her on a journey through a world of bondage, domination, and blood to stop the killer. But can she resist the dark lusts he sparks?

Volume 1 in the Blood & Sex series

Paperback: $12.95

978-1-59003-203-9

Available in August 2010

Blood & Sex: Jonas
by Angela Cameron

Jonas, the strangely appealing owner of the new vampire-themed bondage club could be the perfect distraction for workaholic Dr. Elena Jensen. But their worlds couldn't be farther apart....

Volume 2 of the Blood & Sex series

Paperback: $12.95

978-1-59003-202-2

Available in October 2010

Blood & Sex: Blane
by Angela Cameron

Will Blane be able to break through the guarded reserve of Christiana, the beautiful woman the vampire leader has sent to educate the newest vampires? Or will her sense of duty be stronger than the passion that threatens to sweep her away?

Volume 3 of the Blood & Sex series

Paperback: $12.95

978-1-59003-206-0

Available in December 2010

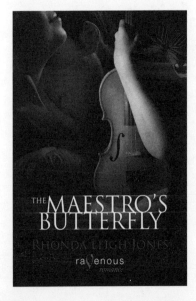

The Maestro's Butterfly
by Rhonda Leigh Jones

Miranda O'Connell has just made a dangerous bet with her mysterious, sexy music teacher that will change her life forever. Will she fall in love with the kinky vampire Maestro and submit to life as a feeder slave? Or will she escape the confines of his estate for the dashing, dangerous charms of his brother?

Paperback: $12.95

978-1-59003-207-7

Available in November 2010

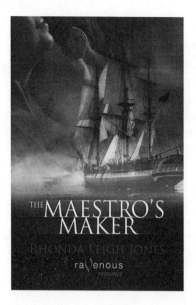

The Maestro's Maker
by Rhonda Leigh Jones

Trapped between two vampires: Chloe discovers the darkness that binds the beautiful and arrogant French noble Claudio du Fresne and his oldest friend Francois Villaforte. With danger, intrigue, and kinky sex, *The Maestro's Maker* takes vampire erotica to passionate new levels!

Paperback: $12.95

978-1-59003-210-7

Available in December 2010

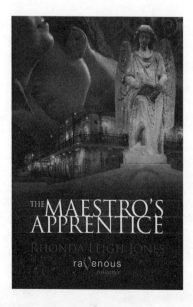

The Maestro's Apprentice
by Rhonda Leigh Jones

For the first time in her life, Autumn is free. She has escaped Claudio du Fresne, the vampire for whom she had been a feeder-slave for years. Now she wants to play, and for her, playing means wild, crazy sex with strangers.

Paperback: $12.95

978-1-59003-209-1

Available in January 2011

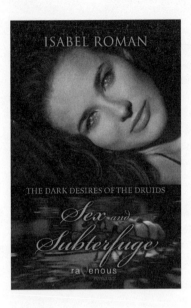

The Dark Desires of the Druids: Sex & Subterfuge
by Isabel Roman

"Do you like jealous heroes and love triangles? How about sizzling sexual encounters atop dining room furniture? If you answered yes to either question, you're going to love this novella." —Susan S., loveromance.passion.com

Paperback: $12.95

978-1-59003-200-8

Available in August 2010

The Dark Desires of the Druids: Desert and Destiny
by Isabel Roman

The first time they met, Arbelle Bahari tried to kill him. The second time, they made love on a desk in the British Museum.

"The action is fast and exciting, the mystery is engaging, and the romance is searingly hot." —*Whipped Cream Reviews* (5 Cherries)

Paperback: $12.95

978-1-59003-201-5

Available in October 2010

Bites of Passion
edited by Cecilia Tan

What does it mean to love a vampire? Does it mean nights of pleasure tempered with sweet pain? Eight top authors explore the themes of immortal love, the lust for blood, and the eternal struggle between light and dark.

Paperback: $12.95

978-1-59003-205-3

Available in September 2010

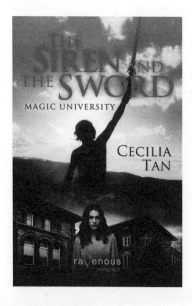

Magic University: The Siren and the Sword
by Cecilia Tan

Harvard freshman Kyle Wadsorth is eager to start a new life. Surprises abound when he discovers a secret magical university hidden inside Harvard and he meets Jess Torralva, who tutors him in the ways of magic, sex, and love.

Paperback: $12.95

978-1-59003-208-4

Available in November 2010

Magic University: The Tower and the Tears by Cecilia Tan

This second volume in the Magic University series brings together myth, magic, and eroticism for adult readers of fantasy who want a bedtime tale of their own.

"Simply one of the most important writers, editors, and innovators in contemporary American erotic literature."—Susie Bright

Paperback: $12.95

978-1-59003-211-4

Available in January 2011

Mind Games by Cecilia Tan

Who hasn't fantasized about using psychic abilities to satisfy your every sexual desire? *Mind Games* provides readers the opportunity to live out that dream....

"Scorching hot with a touch of suspense. Cecilia Tan brings together love, suspense, and scorching sex in a story well worth reading."—*ParaNormal Romance Review*

Paperback: $12.95

978-1-59003-204-6

Available in September 2010